THE LARKVILLE LEGACY

A secret letter...two families changed for ever.

Welcome to the small town of Larkville, Texas, where the Calhoun family has been ranching for generations.

Meanwhile, in New York, the Patterson family rules America's highest echelons of society.

Both families are totally unprepared for the news that they are linked by a shocking secret.

For hidden on the Calhoun ranch is a letter that's been lying unopened and unread—until now!

Meet the two families in all 8 books of this brand-new series:

THE COWBOY COMES HOME
by Patricia Thayer

SLOW DANCE WITH THE SHERIFF
by Nikki Logan

TAMING THE BROODING CATTLEMAN
by Marion Lennox

THE R̲ ̲ ̲ ̲ ̲ ̲S UNEXPECTED FAMILY
̲ ̲na Mackenzie

̲ ̲E CINDERELLA
̲ McClone

̲ ̲GED EVERYTHING
̲don

̲ETHEART

̲BY SOS

Dear Reader

I'm so excited about this series. A new town and family: the Calhouns of Larkville, Texas. It's also been fun working with the other authors on *The Larkville Legacy*. I'm blessed to get to launch the first book, and to get to introduce the founding family of this small ranching town of Larkville.

In my story Clay's daughter, Jess Calhoun, is the single mother of a five-year-old son, Brady, who idolised his Papa Clay and misses him terribly. Jess is dealing with the loss, too. And in her brother's absence she has to run the ranch, which means trying to handle her father's out-of-control stallion Night Storm.

Horse whisperer Johnny Jameson arrives to save the day. The man knows his way around horses a lot better than people. So when his job with troubled equines is finished Johnny always moves on. Yet something about Jess and little Brady has him thinking about staying and putting down roots.

I hope you enjoy my story!

Patricia Thayer

THE COWBOY COMES HOME

BY
PATRICIA THAYER

MILLS & BOON

First published in Great Britain 2012
by Mills & Boon, an imprint of Harlequin (UK) Limited.
Harlequin (UK) Limited, Eton House, 18-24 Paradise Road,
Richmond, Surrey TW9 1SR

© Harlequin Books S.A. 2012

Special thanks and acknowledgement to Patricia Thayer
for her contribution to THE LARKVILLE LEGACY series.

ISBN: 978 0 263 22776 5

Harlequin (UK) policy is to use papers that are natural, renewable
and recyclable products and made from wood grown in sustainable
forests. The logging and manufacturing process conform to the
legal environmental regulations of the country of origin.

Printed and bound in Great Britain
by CPI Antony Rowe, Chippenham, Wiltshire

THE LARKVILLE LEGACY

A secret letter...two families changed for ever.

Welcome to the small town of Larkville, Texas, where the Calhoun family has been ranching for generations.

Meanwhile, in New York, the Patterson family rules America's highest echelons of society.

Both families are totally unprepared for the news that they are linked by a shocking secret.

For hidden on the Calhoun ranch is a letter that's been lying unopened and unread—until now!

Meet the two families in all 8 books of this brand-new series:

Dear Reader

I'm so excited about this series. A new town and family: the Calhouns of Larkville, Texas. It's also been fun working with the other authors on *The Larkville Legacy*. I'm blessed to get to launch the first book, and to get to introduce the founding family of this small ranching town of Larkville.

In my story Clay's daughter, Jess Calhoun, is the single mother of a five-year-old son, Brady, who idolised his Papa Clay and misses him terribly. Jess is dealing with the loss, too. And in her brother's absence she has to run the ranch, which means trying to handle her father's out-of-control stallion Night Storm.

Horse whisperer Johnny Jameson arrives to save the day. The man knows his way around horses a lot better than people. So when his job with troubled equines is finished Johnny always moves on. Yet something about Jess and little Brady has him thinking about staying and putting down roots.

I hope you enjoy my story!

Patricia Thayer

THE COWBOY COMES HOME

BY
PATRICIA THAYER

First published in Great Britain 2012
by Mills & Boon, an imprint of Harlequin (UK) Limited.
Harlequin (UK) Limited, Eton House, 18-24 Paradise Road,
Richmond, Surrey TW9 1SR

© Harlequin Books S.A. 2012

Special thanks and acknowledgement to Patricia Thayer
for her contribution to THE LARKVILLE LEGACY series.

ISBN: 978 0 263 22776 5

Harlequin (UK) policy is to use papers that are natural, renewable and recyclable products and made from wood grown in sustainable forests. The logging and manufacturing process conform to the legal environmental regulations of the country of origin.

Printed and bound in Great Britain
by CPI Antony Rowe, Chippenham, Wiltshire

Originally born and raised in Muncie, Indiana, **Patricia Thayer** is the second of eight children. She attended Ball State University, and soon afterwards headed West. Over the years she's made frequent visits back to the Midwest, trying to keep up with her growing family.

Patricia has called Orange County, California, home for many years. She not only enjoys the warm climate, but also the company and support of other published authors in the local writers' organisation. For the past eighteen years she has had the unwavering support and encouragement of her critique group. It's a sisterhood like no other.

When she's not working on a story, you might find her travelling the United States and Europe, taking in the scenery and doing story research while thoroughly enjoying herself, accompanied by Steve, her husband for over thirty-five years. Together, they have three grown sons and four grandsons. As she calls them: her own true-life heroes. On rare days off from writing you might catch her at Disneyland, spoiling those grandkids rotten! She also volunteers for the Grandparent Autism Network.

Patricia has written for over twenty years, and has authored more than forty-six books. She has been nominated for both a National Readers' Choice Award and the prestigious RITA® Award. Her book NOTHING SHORT OF A MIRACLE won an *RT Book Reviews* Reviewers' Choice award.

A longtime member of Romance Writers of America, she has served as President and held many other board positions for her local chapter in Orange County. She's a firm believer in giving back.

Check her website, www.patriciathayer.com, for upcoming books.

Books by Patricia Thayer

ONCE A COWBOY....*
TALL, DARK, TEXAS RANGER*
THE LONESOME RANCHER*
LITTLE COWGIRL NEEDS A MOM*

The Quilt Shop in Kerry Springs

Did you know these are also available as eBooks?
Visit www.millsandboon.co.uk

To the Gentle Persuaders, Anne, Linda and Linda Mac.

For twenty-two years together,
and if I don't say it enough, thanks for all your support.

CHAPTER ONE

WILLIE NELSON'S "On the Road Again" poured out of the open windows of Johnny Jameson's truck as he drove along the country road. It was January in Texas, but he was energized by the cold air, knowing the temperature would rise to triple digits soon enough come spring. No matter what the weather, he'd much rather be outside than cooped up indoors.

He always liked to keep on the move. Never felt the need to stay at any one place too long. More times than he could count, he had lived out of his vehicle.

He'd been lucky lately. The jobs came to him, and he could pick and choose what he wanted to take on. That was the reason he was coming to Larkville. He'd been intrigued when he'd heard the job description. Also because Clay Calhoun and his prize quarter horses were legendary in Texas. But before he got too excited, he wanted to assess the situation before he made any promises to the man, or to the job. If there still was a job, since the offer had been made months ago.

He'd been delayed by a stubborn colt, but after he'd finished training it, the thoroughbred was worth what the owner had paid. When he'd called Calhoun to let him know he'd be delayed with previous commitments, he'd ended up talking to Clay's son Holt, who'd explained that his father was ill, but assured him that the job would be there whenever he arrived at the ranch. Johnny had said to expect him around the first of the year.

As it turned out it was the first of the year, and he was finally headed for the Double Bar C Ranch. He glanced in the rearview mirror at his trailer, and his precious cargo, Risky Business, his three-year-old roan stallion.

His attention focused back ahead and on the southeast Texas landscape of rolling hills and pastures that had the yellow hue of winter. He looked toward a group of bare trees and a cattle water trough nestled at the base. There was also a visitor, one beautiful black stallion. The animal reared up, fighting to get loose from his lead rope that seemed to be caught on something.

He glanced around to see if anyone was nearby. Not a soul. He pulled his truck to the side of the road and got out. After walking back to check his own horse, he headed toward the open pasture to hopefully save another.

Jess knew she was going to be blamed for this.

Since her brother Holt was away on personal business, her sister, Megan, was away at school and her brother Nate was in the army, she was the one family member around to handle Double Bar C emergencies. Even though she really wasn't involved in the day-to-day running of the ranch—Holt was in charge of that— she knew finding Night Storm had to take top priority.

The bigger problem was, how do you find, much less

bring back, a rogue stallion? No one but Clay Calhoun had ever been able to handle the valuable quarter horse. Now that Dad was gone, the question was what to do with Storm.

The ranch foreman, Wes Brogan, had decided to let the animal out to the fenced pasture, but before Wes was able to transport Storm there, the horse broke away.

When she'd gotten the call early this morning, she immediately went to the barn, saddled up Goldie and rode out to find Storm. She'd been on a horse since she was a baby, so there wasn't any problem keeping up with the ranch hands. To cover more ground, the crew took off in different directions of the vast Calhoun land and so Jess set off on her own.

The Double Bar C had been in the family for generations, and her father had worked hard so it would remain with the Calhouns for many more. Big Clay had loved his horses, especially this stallion, but there had been trouble since Storm had arrived at the ranch. The valuable horse had been mistreated in the past. Eventually Storm began to trust her father somewhat, but since Clay's death a few months back, the horse's behavior had gotten worse and no one had been able to handle him.

She sighed, feeling the bite of the January cold against her cheeks. She slowed her horse as they came to the rise and suddenly caught a spot of black. Taking out her binoculars, she saw the welcome sight.

"Hallelujah!" she cried out, seeing Storm. Then she looked again and saw a man holding on to his lead rope. She didn't recognize him as one of the hands, then she spotted a truck and trailer alongside the road.

"Oh, no, you don't. You're not going to steal Double Bar C property." She kicked her heels into the mare and they shot off.

Johnny had worked with the horse for close to thirty minutes and had made some headway. The animal was still in distress, but at least Johnny had gotten close enough to loop a rope around his neck so he could calm the animal.

And what a beauty he was. His glistening black coat looked well cared for, he thought as he kept the spirited stallion moving in a circle. He pulled the rope taut, knowing he would need an arena to truly work him.

The horse got more agitated when he heard a rider approach, but Johnny couldn't take his attention from his task.

"What do you think you're doing on Calhoun land?"

He was surprised to hear the female voice.

"Trying to help this valuable horse." He managed to maneuver around to see her.

"He's not *your* valuable horse—he belongs to my father."

He noticed the pretty buckskin mare, then he lifted his gaze to the tall blond beauty who sat straight in the saddle. Her long slender legs hugged the animal's flanks and she controlled her horse as if she were born to ride.

"Then maybe I should be having this conversation with Mr. Calhoun."

He heard her gasp, followed by, "That's a little difficult since his death."

Thrown by the news, Johnny slowed the stallion

but when the animal acted up, he turned his attention back to him.

"Please accept my condolences, Ms...."

"Jess Calhoun." She took her lariat off her saddle. "What do you need me to do?"

Back to the problem at hand. "If you can manage it, throw another rope over the stallion's head?" he asked.

"Storm. The horse's name is Night Storm."

She swung the rope overhead and it took a few tries, but she finally hit her target.

Johnny watched as Ms. Calhoun walked her mare backward, pulling the rope tight. That helped to get the animal under control. Somewhat.

"Keep it taut."

She did.

But she also needed questions answered. "Not that I don't appreciate your help, but I have no idea who you are."

"Johnny Jameson. I was on my way to see Clay Calhoun. I had no idea about his death." He wasn't sure what else to say. "I spoke with your father last September in Dallas at a horse auction. He'd asked me to come to the ranch then, but I had a job to finish first and it went on a lot longer than planned." He tugged on the rope. Would this horse ever tire out? "I called Clay right away, but I talked with your brother Holt. He assured me that I'd be welcome whenever I arrived."

He caught the sad emotion that played across her face. "When did Clay pass away?"

"Late October. Pneumonia," she finally said. "He waited too long to see a doctor." She nodded toward the agitated animal. "Storm is Dad's horse. No one else has been able to handle him."

The stallion pawed at the ground and breathed heavily through his nostrils. Johnny tugged on the rope.

Jess watched in amazement. This tall dark stranger sure knew his way around horses. Was Jameson a horse breeder? "Wouldn't want to buy a stallion real cheap, would you?"

He grinned. "Don't be so anxious to get rid of him. Like you said, he's a valuable animal. I think he's also the horse your father wanted me to work with."

Johnny Jameson was dressed in the standard cowboy uniform—jeans and Western-yoked shirt. His wide-brim Stetson shadowed his face, but she could see the chiseled cheekbones and deep-set eyes. When he tipped his head back she caught a glimpse of the gray color of his eyes and felt a tingle of awareness.

No. She wouldn't fall for another cowboy. She took out her cell phone and called Wes. She gave him her location. "More help will be here soon."

They stayed busy with the horse until finally the group of riders came over the hill.

The foreman climbed down from his horse. "Damn, Jess. Your daddy would be proud."

"I didn't do this," she said as one of the men, Will Hinkle, took the rope, relieving her of her job. "Mr. Jameson here caught him."

Wes turned to the man. "I'd shake your hand, but I see you're busy." He paused. "Did you say Jameson? Johnny Jameson?"

"That's me."

The forty-five-year-old Wes grinned. "Well, I'll be damned. You finally made it to our part of Texas."

Jess didn't like being left out. "Finally made it?"

Wes smiled. "Mr. Jameson is one of the top horse trainers around. I remember when Clay got back from Dallas. He was so excited and hopeful about Johnny coming to work with us."

Jameson turned those amazing gray eyes toward her. "Your father and I talked at length. As I said, he's the one who hired me. Thing is, do I still have a job?"

One of the Double Bar C hands drove Johnny's truck to the ranch and gave Johnny the loan of his horse so that he could escort the stallion back personally. It took nearly an hour before Night Storm was back in his stall in the state-of-the-art horse barn at the ranch.

Johnny led the animal inside himself. At least the equine was exhausted from his adventure. And Johnny was hoping he'd be calmer tomorrow so he'd get the chance to work with him.

If he still had the job. Would the pretty Ms. Calhoun override her father and brother's decision?

Once the horse had been fed his special mixture of legumes and oats, Johnny walked outside along with Wes. "That's the calmest I've seen Storm in weeks."

"Is he always so agitated?" Johnny asked.

Wes grew serious. "Pretty much. Clay got him a little over a year ago. He'd been skittish to begin with and we couldn't work out why, then we found the marks on his hind legs."

Johnny had missed those. Usually there was something that caused a horse to be distraught, leery. And abuse was often a big factor.

"Clay was the one who handled him, but Storm could still be unpredictable. It's gotten worse since Clay's not around anymore. That's why I let him out to graze this morning." Wes tipped his hat back. "You saw how that worked out. So you think you can help him?"

He liked a challenge. He wanted to prove, especially to the abuser, that Storm could be turned around. "All I promise is that I'll try. That is, if Ms. Calhoun wants me to handle Storm's training."

"It's not my decision one way or the other," the familiar woman's voice said.

They both turned to see Jess.

Johnny was still awestruck by her beauty. Tall and slender with those mile-long legs encased in formfitting jeans. She brushed the single braid off her shoulder and walked toward them.

Good. He wanted to get a closer look. His gaze moved over her and he wasn't disappointed. Her skin was flawless and her large eyes were a golden-brown in color. His attention went to her mouth, and those full lips. He swallowed at the sudden dryness in his throat.

Okay, you'd better concentrate on business.

"I can't thank you enough for what you did today, Mr. Jameson. If you have an agreement with my brother, of course you have a job here."

"It was an understanding," he admitted. "I'll need an agreement in writing for my fees and my training style."

Jess started to speak, but Wes said, "Jess, why don't we phone Holt." He turned to Johnny. "Holt is away on personal business. You wouldn't mind waiting a few minutes while we speak to him, would you?"

"Not a problem. I'll go see to my horse."

Jess watched the familiar cowboy's swagger as he walked away. Raised on a ranch, she'd known many men like him. Good-looking, sweet-talking, love 'em and leave 'em. His way, his game, then pack up and hit the road.

She had been uncomfortable with the way Johnny Jameson looked at her. It was a good thing that she didn't have any part in running the ranch. Except when her big brother went out of town and she was the only one to handle it.

Wes stopped just inside the barn. "Jess, you are going to hire Johnny?"

She shook her head, knowing she had power of attorney while Holt was away. "Of course, but I'd feel better talking to Holt first since we have to agree to the money and terms."

Wes nodded, took out his cell phone and punched in the call button for Holt. Once the foreman finished with his questions, Jess asked her brother a few of her own. Satisfied, she agreed to what the trainer would need and that he would sign a contract. She hung up and smiled at Wes.

"Looks like we have a trainer for Storm."

They headed back through the barn. She had just agreed to pay a hefty fee to Mr. Jameson.

"Seems like a lot for a trainer," she remarked.

Wes nodded. "A trainer as good as Johnny Jameson can name his price." Wes stopped. "Look, Jess. I know you haven't been around the operation, and if you had, you'd know that the vet has been out several times to medicate Storm. Doc Peters has talked about the possibility of putting him down."

Jess gasped. "We wouldn't do that!"

"Of course not," Wes agreed. "He's a valuable animal, but he's also out of control right now. We can't ride him or breed him when he's like this."

"But Storm was dad's horse."

"And that's the reason Holt's put up with his behavior these past months. But someone could get hurt. Jameson is our best hope. It's the right decision to hire him."

Jess knew after just one meeting that the man had stirred something in her. That was the problem. She felt the attraction. Bad news. She also couldn't forget her lousy track record with men.

At least she didn't need to be around that much, and her home and business were on another part of the ranch. That made her a little more relaxed until she walked out of the barn and caught the scene in the corral unfolding before her. She could only watch as Johnny lifted her four-year-old son to the railing. She stiffened, seeing how animated Brady was with the new trainer as his small hand reached out toward the forehead of the man's roan horse. Quickly the boy pulled his hand back and laughed nervously. Jess hadn't heard that sound since before Brady's grandfather had died. Wasn't her son afraid of horses? She remembered that day when Brady had been barely two years old, and he'd gone with his grandpa Clay to the barn and a horse broke away and nearly knocked him down. From then on, her son had cried every time her dad tried to take him back to the barn.

Now, Brady was trusting a stranger.

"Well, looks like Brady likes him," Wes remarked. "You know what they say."

"About what?"

"You got to trust a man who's liked by animals and children."

Brady Clayton Calhoun ran over to her. "Mom, I did it! I petted him."

"I see that."

She looked down at her blond-headed son. So much pride in his big brown eyes.

"I wasn't scared. Johnny said that Risky would never hurt me." A big smile crossed his face. "And he didn't."

"You did a great job." She hugged him. "Brady, why don't you go up to the house? I bet Nancy's finished baking those cookies."

The boy started off, then stopped. "Are you coming, too, Mom?"

"I'll be there shortly, son. I have some business to talk over with Mr. Jameson." Johnny was approaching her and Wes.

"'Kay." Then Brady ran off through the gate.

Jess turned to Johnny. "I'm not sure how you got him to do that, but I'd appreciate it if you'd check with me before you introduce my child to any of the animals."

"Yes, ma'am." He nodded. "You're the boss."

Jess wasn't sure how to react to Johnny Jameson. She'd never been good at flirting with men. Okay, maybe once, and that had gotten her into trouble. She definitely had no idea how to judge men.

"No, Mr. Jameson, I'm not." She wished Wes hadn't left her alone to handle this. "Holt's still happy to hire you. But until he returns, you'll answer to the ranch foreman. If something comes up that Wes questions, then we'll discuss it."

"So you aren't the least bit interested in how Storm progresses?"

"Of course I am, but I have other things that take up my time."

Jameson's gray eyes bored into her, causing a stirring inside her that not only surprised but frightened her. Feelings she thought had been dormant for a long time. For the past nearly five years her child and her business had filled all the voids. Now this man was creating something she didn't want or need.

She pulled her jacket together to ward off the cold. "So if there's nothing else, I need to get inside."

"Nothing I can't handle. Sorry I took up so much of your time." He placed two fingers against the brim of his hat in a salute. "Good afternoon, Ms. Calhoun."

"Mr. Jameson."

"Why don't you just call me Johnny? Unless you don't like to get that familiar with the hired help."

She refused to react. "I'm familiar with a lot of the men who work on the Double Bar C. I've known some all my life, but I don't know you."

He smiled. "Yet."

Jess nodded and turned toward the house, trying to keep her walk slow and relaxed, but Johnny Jameson had managed to knock her off balance. She couldn't

allow that. She had once and soon learned that trusting a man led to hurt and pain. *No, Mr. Good-Looking
Cowboy, I'm not falling for your type again.*

CHAPTER TWO

AN HOUR later, Jess was standing in the ranch kitchen, looking out toward the corral, watching as the new trainer carried his things up the steps to the apartment above the barn.

Johnny Jameson was moving in. For how long? Would he just work with Storm, or would Holt keep him here longer?

She shook away the questions. What did it matter? Once her brother came home, he'd handle the ranch again. And she'd go back to concentrating on her business, which she'd been neglecting the past weeks.

No doubt about it, even months later the entire family was struggling to adjust to all the changes since her father's death.

Now, Holt was away, taking care of a terminally ill friend. Megan was at school in the East. Nate was in the army.

She released a sigh. The ranch problems were hers to deal with. Her immediate choice had been to hire a horse trainer. Well, she'd have to wait and see how that worked out.

She turned around and saw her son at the big oak table, eating an afternoon snack. A sudden sadness consumed her. Her father used to wander in about this time of day and join his grandson for milk and cookies. She could still hear Brady's giggles and her father's laughter ring out through the house.

Clay Calhoun's death had been hard on all of them, but mostly her son. The twosome had been inseparable. The only exception had been when it came to horses. Her father always thought Brady would outgrow his fears, but didn't push the issue. That was why she had been so surprised when the child showed up in the corral today.

Jess still worried about her son. Not an outgoing boy by nature, the soon-to-be five-year-old needed to interact more with his peers. So three mornings a week Brady had been attending preschool while she ran her store, Jess's Bakery, featuring homemade preserves, which she'd named after her mother: Sandra's Preserves.

"Mom, is Johnny staying here for a long time?"

She studied Brady's brown eyes. "Not sure, honey. He's going to work with Grandpa's horse."

The boy took a drink of milk, then said, "'Cause Storm is sad about Papa going to heaven?"

She smiled. "Yeah, Storm is sad, too." Was that the reason she resented Johnny, an outsider, coming here? Because he could handle her dad's horse so easily, when none of them could? Or that her son trusted him?

"I hope he can make Storm happy again," Brady said.

"So do I, son." She turned back around and looked out the row of windows toward the horse barn. "For what we're paying him, he'd better," she murmured.

Jess hated this. Since her dad's death, Holt had taken over the running of the ranch as if he'd been born to it. He had been, but he wasn't here and could be away a long time. In the past, she'd always gone to her dad for answers and now he wasn't around any longer.

She felt the sting of tears, remembering back six years ago when she'd told her parents she was pregnant and was going to be a single mom.

Even though her mother voiced her disappointment, her dad wrapped her in his big strong arms and told her that it would be all right. He made sure of that. The moment her son was born, Clay claimed him as a Calhoun. Over the years, it had been her dad who taught her about the importance of the land and family.

She turned back to her child. "Brady, what made you go into the corral today?"

The boy shrugged, concentrating on his chocolate chip cookie. "I dunno."

"I thought we talked about this. Until you're older, you need an adult to be with you when you're around the stock. Please, pay attention to the rules. They're for your safety."

He looked at her. "I came to find you. I was afraid you got hurt 'cause of Storm." She saw the fear in his eyes.

She went to him at the table and knelt down. "Honey, I wouldn't get close to a runaway horse on my own. And Wes was there, too."

"And so was Johnny. Papa said he can work miracles."

Oh, no, was he making things up? "Brady, we talked about this. Papa Clay is gone away."

"I know. He's buried in the ground on the hill with Grandma Sandy." He pointed toward the barn. "But Papa said this before, when he was sick in bed. 'Member when I went to his room and read him stories? Sometimes he talked about the ranch."

She couldn't hide her smile. That sounded like Dad. "I think you better talk to Holt about that."

"Papa already told Uncle Holt that he needed to teach me 'cause I hafta know how to run the Double Bar C when I grow up and be the boss. That's when Papa and Uncle Holt talked about Johnny." Brady wrinkled his freckled nose. "Mom, did you know that he talks to horses?"

"Who, Papa?"

"No, Johnny. And that's why Papa wanted him to come here." Tears formed in the child's eyes. "That's why I had to go and see Johnny. To tell him things about Storm."

Jess blinked several times. "Okay." She hugged him. He'd been so tough through the past months. "But next time let an adult know before you head to the corral. Storm isn't safe to be around."

"I know. But now Johnny's gonna fix Storm so he's a nice horse."

From a child's mouth to God's ears. "We all want that, son, and I hope it happens, but don't expect miracles."

"But there are miracles, Mom. In Sunday school they talk about them all the time."

Okay, she was going to lose this one. "Okay, we'll see what happens."

"So, can I watch Johnny with Storm?"

She shook her head. "It's too dangerous right now."

"What if Johnny says it's okay, then can I do it?"

She was torn. Brady had been so afraid to get anywhere close to the stables. Now he wanted to be around the orneriest horse ever. "All right, when we see Johnny again, we'll talk about it."

He cheered. "Tonight."

"Tonight?"

He nodded. "I asked him to come to supper, and he said yes."

Great. She didn't need this now, didn't need to face Johnny again so soon.

She nodded and he climbed down from the table and ran off.

Nancy came in and cleared the table. "That's a first, the boy going anywhere near a horse."

Jess glanced at the housekeeper and nodded. "It shocked me, all right."

"I can't wait to get a good look at this Johnny Jameson."

In her mid-forties, Nancy Griffith was full-figured. She had light brown hair that she wore pulled back into a ponytail, and had pretty hazel eyes and a smile that was as warm as she was herself. And since Jess's mother died a few years ago, they had become the best of friends.

"Well, you can stroll down to the barn if you like."

The housekeeper smiled. "I'll just wait until supper."

Jess thought about the man. She knew his type—he attracted women, and probably didn't get turned down much. Well, she wasn't going to be affected by him. "Nancy would you mind watching Brady for a while?"

"Of course not."

"Good, I'm going to head back to the bakery for a few hours. I have my own business to run." Before that she needed to show some Texas hospitality.

Johnny finished bringing his things upstairs to the two-room apartment. There was a living area and small kitchen. The other room held a queen-size bed and dresser. There was a tiny bathroom, with no tub, but a shower stall. That was plenty for him.

He sank into the well-worn leather sofa. Home. Until… At least for a few weeks. Not much longer than that. He'd always moved on when the mood struck him. He never wanted to get too attached to a place, especially when he felt he didn't fit in. That was most of the time.

Yet, this ranch was a top-quality facility. Large stalls, a well-ventilated barn. Clay Calhoun had been serious about his horses.

He sank farther into the cushions. The past few years, he'd made good money because of his training skills. Moving around, he'd banked most of it. He'd invested some in stocks, and some in horses. Risky Business was his latest find. The previous owner deemed the young stallion untrainable and dangerous. Johnny got him at a steal. After a lot of patience and training, Risky had turned into a great horse. Johnny had even bred him. He thought back to the sweet mare that Jess Calhoun rode today. The two would produce a fine-looking foal.

His thoughts wandered toward Ms. Calhoun. She was one pretty woman. Not your typical rich rancher's daughter. She'd ridden out on a cold January day to find her dad's horse just like the hired hands.

She went by the name Calhoun and had a son, so was she divorced, or never married? Either way, he needed to stay clear of her. A woman with a child wasn't a good thing. Not for him. He'd never fit into that mold. He flashed back to years ago, to his mother and her crazy boyfriend with the freewheeling fist. Nope, he didn't do the family or commitment thing. He'd heard the word *love* tossed around enough to know that it had been meaningless to him. It had only been connected to hurtful memories. With love came trust, and it was hard to trust someone when they were beating the hell out of you.

But damn, Jess Calhoun was tempting enough to make him forget a lot of pain.

There was a knock at the door. "Come in."

The door opened and Jess stuck her head in. "I wanted to bring by some sheets and towels. We didn't know you were coming, so your bed isn't made up."

When he looked at her, he didn't think about making up a bed. He stood. "It's okay. I kind of sprung my arrival on you."

"Not a problem. Storm needs help." She nodded and glanced around nervously. "I hope the accommodations are satisfactory for you."

If she'd only seen some of the places he'd lived in.

"I didn't expect anything besides a bed in the bunkhouse. This is great."

Johnny took the linens from her. Their hands brushed and he felt her jump. "Well, we want you to be comfortable."

"I am, thank you." He paused and rushed on to say, "Again, I want to apologize for letting Brady pet Risky earlier. I trust my horse, so I never once thought he might hurt the boy."

She nodded. "I know I'm a little overprotective. I'm not used to Brady going to strangers, especially around horses."

He couldn't help but be intrigued by this woman's situation. "What about Brady's father?"

She glanced away. "He's not in his life."

Johnny felt his chest tighten. He knew what it was like to have no father. "I'm sorry."

She sighed. "Some things are for the best. That was one of the reasons why my father and Brady were so close. We've all suffered greatly since his death."

"I can understand that," he told her. "I promise I won't do anything to upset Brady. I only want to help Storm."

"Good. I should go and let you get settled in."

She headed for the door when Wes appeared. "Looks like I'm a little late for the welcoming committee."

Jess nodded. "I'm leaving, so you can continue for me." She was gone.

Wes stayed. "I just talked with Holt again," the foreman said. "He told me to make sure you feel at home. So whatever you need let me know."

"Everything is fine."

Wes grinned. "We want to make sure you hang around for a while."

"No promises. I agreed to work with Storm, but after that, we'll see."

"Fair enough." Wes opened the door to leave.

"Supper is at six. See you then."

Johnny wasn't going to barge in on the Calhouns. "Look, Wes. I don't have to go. I know the boy extended the invite but..."

"And Brady will probably have a million questions for you." Wes paused. "Look, as you can see the boy has a big fear of horses mainly because of an incident with a spooked horse when he was a toddler. He's really looking forward to talking to you at supper." The foreman frowned. "And if the boy is taking an interest in you training Storm, I take it as a good sign."

Johnny finally nodded. As long as the boy didn't expect anything more than a few answers about horses. "I guess I can handle as many questions as he can ask."

A smile spread across Wes's face. "I suggest you stick around long enough to sample Jess's dessert. That's her specialty."

The picture in Johnny's head conjured a lot more than sweet confections. "Then I guess I should stay and have a taste."

Johnny studied the big ranch-style house, which might have been built a hundred years ago. There had been several additions to the structure, including the large kitchen that had been remodeled recently with all the modern conveniences. There was a huge double oven and the gas cooktop had eight burners. The refrigerator was industrial-size. Then he learned that Jess's late mother, Sandra, and Jess had begun making their homemade jellies and jams right here until Jess had outgrown the space. After her mother's heart attack and death three years ago, Jess had opened up shop at another location on the ranch.

So Ms. Calhoun worked for a living.

The group sat in front of the fireplace at a long wooden table that looked as if it had been around for years. Wes explained that Clay had liked eating in the kitchen.

Although the Calhouns were extremely wealthy you couldn't tell by the way they acted or treated others. They were down-to-earth folk.

The meal was pot roast with potatoes and carrots. His favorite. The biscuits were mouthwatering. And, oh, yeah, he couldn't wait until dessert.

"What do you whisper to the horses?" Brady asked, breaking into his thoughts. "Magic words?"

"No, not magic. I just want to get the horse used to my voice. Not spook 'em. Each animal is different." He glanced across the table at Jess. "Sometimes, if it's a filly, I've been known to sweet-talk them. All females respond to that."

The boy giggled. "Mom likes it when I'm sweet, too."

Jess smiled at her son.

Brady turned back to him. "Can I watch you train Storm? Mom said I have to ask permission."

Johnny glanced at Jess again. He wasn't sure how she felt about it. "Why don't you give me a little time with him and we'll see how it goes? Horses can be unpredictable."

The boy frowned. "I don't know what that word means."

"It means we don't know how Storm will act. He

misses your grandfather. And from what I've been told they were good friends. I'm gonna try and help him so he'll trust people."

"You think someday I can pet him like I did Risky?"

"That's what I'm hoping for."

When Nancy stood and began to clear the table, Wes immediately got up and helped her. Johnny smiled as the two huddled together at the sink and talked quietly.

The boy leaned toward him and cupped his small hand to his mouth. "Wes's sweet on Nancy."

"Brady," his mother called. "You shouldn't whisper at the table, it's impolite."

"Sorry, Mom."

She nodded and glanced at the clock. "I think it's about time we head home. So go gather your things. You have school tomorrow."

The kid opened his mouth, then closed it. He turned to Johnny. "Papa Clay said that a gentleman never sasses a lady."

"Your grandfather was a smart man."

"The smartest in the whole wide world." The boy got up from the table and walked out.

The room grew silent except for the soft tones coming from the other side of the kitchen. "I should go, too," he told Jess.

He was surprised when she reached across the table and touched his arm to stop him. He felt the warmth of her delicate hand through his shirt.

"Please, don't leave." She quickly moved it away. "I mean, finish your coffee, Mr. Jameson. And have some dessert. It's apple pie."

He looked into those light brown eyes. "I will if you stop calling me mister. Again, the name is Johnny."

"Johnny," she repeated. "And I'm Jess."

"That short for Jessica?"

With her nod, he said, "I think Jess suits you better."

"I don't know if I should ask what you mean by that."

"I'd say you're a solid, dependable person."

She quickly changed the subject. "What about you, Johnny Jameson? Do you have a place you call home?"

He hated to have the tables turned on him. But it was best she knew him from the start. No surprises. "No. I travel too much with my work to pay for a place that would be empty for months at a time. As you can see, my trailer is big enough." He smiled. "And a pretty good sleeping quarters, and just about everything else I need."

"You don't get lonely?"

Hell, he'd been lonely all his life. He took a sip of coffee. "I've been on my own since I was a kid. I like moving around from place to place." He needed to get her away from talking about him. "Enough about me." He leaned forward, his voice low. "I'd rather talk about a pretty woman, with a smile that could stop a man in his tracks."

A blush rose on her cheeks and she glanced away.

"Too much information?" he asked.

"Maybe a little inappropriate. We don't even know each other."

He started to speak when he heard a familiar voice ask, "Mom, what does inppro...inpprop...?"

Smiling, Johnny stood. "It means that I didn't behave myself, son." He ruffled the boy's hair and walked to the back door. Grabbing his hat off the hook he looked back at the woman he suspected would be keeping him awake tonight.

"Good night, Jess. Brady." He turned and walked out into the cold, but that didn't put out the fire in his belly.

The next morning, Jess had struggled to get Brady dressed and out the door on time. She needed to open the store. Her manager and right-hand man, Molly Dayton, usually came in early on Brady's school days to start the baking orders.

With ten minutes to spare she kissed her son good-bye at preschool, then climbed into her small silver SUV and drove back two miles toward the west side of the ranch. To the section of Calhoun land that ran next to the highway and the home of Jess's bakery. Above the shop was also a two-bedroom apartment where she and Brady called home.

Even though the bakery had been a dream of hers none of it would have come to be if not for her father. He'd convinced her to keep going after what she wanted in life.

When she'd outgrown the kitchen at the ranch for jarring the fruit preserves, and the mail-order business took off for Sandra's jellies and preserves, he'd loaned her the money for a bakery with a small warehouse at the back to expand her business.

She'd talked him into adding a two-bedroom apartment over the bakery so she and Brady had their own place.

Clay had complained about her living so far away from the main house, but there were two shifts a day with production in the warehouse, so there needed to be someone close by. Right now the store didn't get as much traffic as she wanted; most of her jelly and jam sales were from the internet. She hoped to change that. She didn't want to live over the bakery permanently. That was why she had more plans to expand, not only the business but her home.

Jess parked at the side of the building and walked through the front door of the store. The familiar aroma of the baking bread and cakes hit her as she went behind the long counter to the cash register. She took out the bills and coins from her purse and added them to the cash register for today's sales.

Removing her coat, she walked along the high glass case filled with sweets, cakes and pies that were fresh for today's customers.

The entire store was filled with her products. The shelves along the opposite wall were stacked with Sandra's Preserves. During the winter months, she didn't expect a lot of traffic in the store, but they were still busy filling orders from town.

Jess heard a familiar voice from the back and looked up to see her best friend carrying in a tray of cakes.

"Hi, Mol."

"Morning, Jess."

Molly Dayton had lived in Larkville all her life. That was how long she'd been friends with Jess. Molly had moved to Houston for college, and a few years ago when her parents had lost their ranch, she'd come home to help out. Now, her father, Ben, handled the shipping of all the bakery's products. Molly's mother, Carol, was her best baker. All ten of her employees were the best.

"Did Jerry deliver the café's order?" Jess asked.

"Yes, even Mrs. Fielder's birthday cake made it on the truck." Molly set the tray down on the counter. It was laden with two carrot cakes and three of her double Dutch chocolate cakes. Jess smiled. "Looks like your mother's been busy."

The pretty brunette smiled. "Hey, be careful, or she'll take over."

Jess loved Carol Dayton. She had come in to help with her quickly expanding business, and now, Jess didn't know what she'd do without her. "How is everything else going?"

Molly folded her arms. "You tell me, friend."

"What happened?"

"A good-looking guy shows up at your ranch and I have to hear about it in town."

CHAPTER THREE

JESS should have realized how fast word traveled in Larkville. With the population less than two thousand, everyone knew everyone else. A stranger coming to town was big news.

"I take it you're talking about Johnny Jameson."

"There's another good-looking cowboy in Larkville?"

"Not that I've been looking, but I'd say there are several, especially with early-spring roundup coming soon."

Molly opened the case and placed two cakes on the shelf. She paused and looked at Jess. "It's a shame you have such a cynical outlook on men. It might be fun to fight you for him."

Jess straightened. "This isn't high school. If you're interested in Johnny, go for it."

Molly nodded. "Okay, I'm curious to know what he looks like. Maybe you can invite me to the ranch for supper and have this Johnny Jameson come, too?"

Jess didn't want to spend any more time with the man than she had to. "Wouldn't that be a little obvious?"

"Maybe, but there aren't a lot of single men around here to choose from. The good ones seem to all be married, or they're ranch hands and move around a lot. The last guy I dated seemed to have more loyalty to his horse than to me. And then he took off. I'm looking for a stick-around guy."

Weren't they all, Jess thought. "Well, don't look at Johnny for stability. He's got his truck, trailer and his trusty horse. Horse Trainer Will Travel seems to be his motto."

Molly shrugged. "Maybe he hasn't met the right woman, yet."

Jess would hate to see her friend hurt again. One of the reasons Molly came back to Larkville had been because of a man who wouldn't commit. And Jess knew all about that type of man. "Mol, just tread carefully."

Her friend eyed her closely. "And you're too careful, Jess. At least I'm out there trying to find love. It's better than what you do, hide out from life."

She glanced around the bakery. "You call this hiding out? Besides, I'm a little busy with a son and running a business."

Molly gave her an incredulous look. "You have no idea how men look at you. Just about any male in town would swallow his tongue if you showed him some interest."

Jess knew about some of them. "Most are far too old, and some of the others just like the fact that I'm Clay Calhoun's daughter." She had Brady to think about, too. "I never know if the interest is in me, or the Calhoun fortune."

"Then go somewhere that's never heard of Clay Calhoun."

Jess smiled. "I guess I'd have to leave Texas, huh?"

Molly laughed. "Okay, I see your point." Her friend grew serious again. "I know Chad did a number on you. He's lower than a snake for walking away when you were pregnant. But, Jess, you can't give up on finding that great guy."

Jess stiffened. She'd heard this story before, and she could always push it off before when Brady had Papa Clay to take care of him. But now the man in both their lives was gone.

Jess didn't want to deal with this now. "Why do you feel the need to give me this same pep talk about every six months?"

"Because I hate to see you close yourself up. Not all men are like your ex."

"Chad never made me any promises."

"Well, you should expect promises and more. So good riddance to him."

The jingle of the bell rang over the bakery door. Thank God, a customer. She sent Molly back into the kitchen and went off to sell her goods.

She had her work and her son. That was enough for her. But was it enough for Brady?

Johnny had spent his first morning, along with a couple of the ranch hands, setting up a temporary sixty-foot round pen.

Once it was completed, he worked Storm for about an hour. This was only their second time together, and they needed to get used to each other. The stallion was leery—the pinned-back ears, the cocking of his hind leg whenever Johnny had gotten close. Storm's body language said it all. Stay away.

Seemed similar to the signals Jess Calhoun gave him.

He shook off the mental interruption and put his concentration back on the horse.

After he'd finished with Storm, Johnny took the animal back to his stall, then drove into Larkville. He needed a break and to do some shopping to stock up on food. Most of all he wanted to get a look around. He'd never been to this part of east Texas. When he came off the highway he wasn't surprised to see how small the town was. After all, it was a ranching community.

History had it the town had been founded by cattle baron William Scout Calhoun, who'd settled in Hayes County in the nineteenth century. Johnny read it on a plaque at the edge of Washington Park just before the center of town. Seemed that the next generations of Calhouns continued the tradition and made their money in cattle.

Johnny pulled into the lone gas station in town, Gus's Fillin' Station. He got out to pump as an older man came rushing out of the small building with a big smile. "Howdy."

"Hello," Johnny returned.

The man looked to be about sixty and walked with a lazy gait. His face was weather-beaten and a battered straw cowboy hat covered thin gray hair.

He took the nozzle from the holder and began pumping gas. "Fill 'er up?"

Johnny nodded. "Sure."

"So, you stayin' in town awhile?"

"Depends on how fast I can do my job."

"I hear you're the fancy horse trainer that Clay hired."

It had been only twenty-four hours since his arrival in town and already the news of his arrival had spread. "I guess you heard right. I'm a horse trainer, and Clay Calhoun hired me."

The guy nodded and held out his hand. "Gus Everett."

He shook it. "Johnny Jameson."

"Good to meet you, Johnny. If I'd been Clay I would have put that good-for-nothin' horse out of its misery a long time ago. But that wasn't Clay. He loved that black devil of a stallion." The old man shook his head and Johnny could see the sadness in his eyes. "Damn, I miss that old cuss. Best friend a man could ask for."

"I've been hearing that a lot."

"Take it as gospel, son."

Gus also shared the history of the Calhouns. The founding family had made a fortune in breeding stock and horses, but also in oil. They had made good investments that helped ward off drought and low beef prices. They still ran a sizable mixed Angus and Hereford herd on Calhoun land.

After Johnny had finally gotten away from Gus, he drove to a mom-and-pop grocery store called the Smart Mart to pick up some staples—bread, milk and some lunch meat for sandwiches. He walked up and down the four short aisles, pushing his cart past the limited selection. He turned a corner and found a pleasant surprise. *Well, well, Ms. Jess Calhoun shops, too.*

He couldn't help but stare. The woman was beautiful. Her hair was tied back in her usual braid, showing off her delicate bone structure and flawless skin. Her eyes had caught his attention yesterday. Although she was looking away, he'd memorized the color. Aged whiskey came to mind. She bent over and his gaze moved over her dark slacks that covered her shapely hips and legs. Oh, yeah, someone like Jess could get your blood going on a cold morning.

"Excuse me, would you know where the mustard is?"

She turned around. "Oh, Johnny," she gasped, and the sound conjured up a whole different scenario.

"Sorry, I didn't mean to startle you."

"You didn't, I just didn't expect to see you here."

"Men have to shop, too."

"Of course." She glanced down at his cart. "Are you getting settled in?"

"Yes, I got just what I need here."

She put on a smile. "Good. How is Storm today?"

"Ornery as ever."

This time her smile was genuine. "Sorry. He isn't going to be easy to train. You're going to have your hands full."

"That's why you pay me. I do the hard jobs."

Jess wasn't sure what was keeping her asking questions. She really didn't need to get friendly with another drifting cowboy. When she looked him in the eyes it was as if she was mesmerized. Not good.

She started pushing her cart to one of the two checkouts. She went to one and Johnny went to the other.

Somehow they ended up walking outside the store together. She spoke to people passing by on the main street. They openly eyed Johnny and she did some quick introductions.

"This is a friendly town," Johnny said.

She nodded as they walked to the parking lot, which happened to be the one that all the downtown stores used. "Larkville is small, but we have pretty much what we need."

She nodded across the street. "Hal's Drug and Photo. You can get a prescription while your pictures are developed."

"Convenient."

"Our town hall." She pointed to the two-story stone building. "Our mayor is Johanna Hollis—she was just elected this past year. It took a lot to get a woman in office. Farther down the street is the Lone Star Mercantile. If you need a pair of jeans, or a saddle, that's where you'd go."

Johnny looked up and down the two-lane street as if he were searching for something. "Is there a good place to eat?"

"That would be Gracie May's Diner. Best coffee around."

"How about lunch?"

She nodded. "The food is good, too."

He smiled and it did funny things to her stomach. "What I meant, Jess, is would you have lunch with me?"

"Oh, I can't." She shook her head quickly, trying to think up an excuse. "I have to pick up Brady from school."

"Then bring him along. I want to thank you for having me to supper last night."

"That's not necessary. Really."

He gave a sly smile. "Surely you aren't going to let me eat alone."

She knew this man didn't need her sympathy. Any

woman would be willing to go, including her, she had to admit. "Okay, give me fifteen minutes to get Brady from school. I'll meet you there." Jess walked away, fighting the need to run. To run far from this man and the feelings he'd created in her.

After getting Brady from preschool, Jess walked him to Gracie May's. She hated that she felt nervous. When had been the last time she'd had lunch with a man? High school?

Most of all she didn't want Brady getting too attached to Johnny. Maybe that was why she hadn't explained the plan to meet Johnny for lunch to her son. The child was already intrigued by the man. Suddenly Brady had an interest in horses, but it seemed to be also about the man.

"Mom, can I have French fries?"

She'd rather he ate something healthier, but said, "This once."

She opened the door to the old storefront diner and looked around. It had been built in the fifties and not much had changed. It had worn linoleum floors and cracked red vinyl-covered booths. A lunch counter ran along the length of the restaurant, and every stool was filled. The place was crowded for lunch. Good. Several customers were eating her pies.

She glanced around for her lunch date. No, it wasn't a date, she chided herself. She finally found Johnny sitting in a booth along the window.

"Mom, Johnny's here."

"I see that."

They both walked over as Johnny stood next to his table. "Hi, Brady."

"Hi, Johnny. Are we going to have lunch with you?"

"I'd like it if you two would join me."

Brady looked at her. "Sure."

Once again, she was surprised by her son's enthusiasm. "Hello, Jess."

"Johnny."

He took her coat and hung it up on the hook at the end of the booth.

"I want to sit with Johnny," Brady said, and climbed into the seat by the window. Jess sat down across from them.

"Did you see Storm today?" the child asked.

"Yes, I did. I worked with him this morning."

"Did you hear that, Mom?"

"That's good, because that's Johnny's job," she said, then looked at Johnny. With his hat off, she could really notice his eyes. Those light gray eyes. "Is he any better?"

"Not yet. It's going to take a while."

The waitress, Bonnie Waters, came by with two cups and a coffeepot. "Well, what do we have here?" She filled the mugs.

Jess put on a smile. "Bonnie, this is Johnny Jameson, the new trainer who is working with Storm."

The fortysomething woman stood back and took stock of the man. "Either you're just plain crazy, or you're really good at what you do." She smiled. "Since you're so good to look at, I don't care which it is. Welcome to Larkville, Johnny Jameson."

Johnny gave her a smile. "Thank you, Bonnie. I hear the food here is pretty good."

The waitress winked at Jess. "Well, I can guarantee the dessert is."

"That's 'cause it's my mom's," Brady said as he got up on his knees.

"You're a good son, Mr. Brady Calhoun," Bonnie said. "So what's your pleasure today?"

"I want a hamburger and French fries."

"I'll have the same," Johnny added.

"Me, too," Jess finished.

The waitress walked away and Brady took over the conversation, wanting to know everything that Johnny did with Storm.

"I was telling your mother that he's getting used to me."

"Will that take a long time?"

Johnny glanced at Jess, not knowing how to answer the boy. "I'm hoping not too long."

"So this is why you sneaked off today?"

Johnny looked over his shoulder and found a pretty brunette standing at the end of the booth, smiling. She had dark eyes that revealed her interest in him.

"Hi, Aunt Molly," Brady cheered. "This is Johnny. He's helping Papa's horse."

The brunette nodded. "Horse trainer extraordinaire." Before any introduction could be made, she stuck out her hand. "Hello, I'm Molly Dayton."

Johnny stood. "Johnny Jameson. Pleased to meet you, Molly."

"I'd say the pleasure is mine."

Jess drew her attention momentarily. "Molly, please join us for lunch."

Jess slid over and Molly sat down beside her. "So, Johnny Jameson, I've heard a lot about you."

Johnny was surprised. "You have?"

"Small town, you know. Also Jess here is my best friend. But she is a little on the serious side."

Johnny laughed. "Something tells me you've spent a lot of years trying to change that."

They both laughed. Jess sat up straight and said, "Hello, I'm right here."

Molly grinned. "And she's fun to tease."

"And I'm also your boss," Jess said. "And I don't have time today. I need to get Brady back to the ranch before long, then I have a meeting with a prospective retailer."

Molly gasped. "The Good Neighbor grocery chain is going to carry your jams and jellies?"

Jess hesitated. "Nothing definite, but keep your fingers crossed."

"I'll do better than that," Molly said. "I'll run Brady back to the ranch for you. But I'll need to borrow your car seat."

"Mol, I don't want you to go all the way out there." She had trouble focusing with Johnny Jameson across from her.

"Not a problem." Her friend glanced at Johnny, giving him the once-over. "I wouldn't mind seeing you at work."

Brady's head snapped up at her. "Mom, I want to watch Johnny, too."

Jess tried not to react to Molly's flirting. "Sorry, son,

too dangerous. You need to stay inside with Nancy. I mean it."

Brady didn't look happy.

"How about this, Brady," Johnny began. "Why don't you and Molly show me around town after lunch?"

The child still didn't look happy. "Okay."

Jess still didn't like this situation any better. But by the looks of things, she'd been outmaneuvered.

"Just behave." She wasn't sure if she was talking to her son or her friend.

Later on that day, after spending an hour or so in town with Brady and Molly, Johnny returned to the Double Bar C Ranch and approached Storm's stall. Already he heard the horse's high-pitched whinnies and the sound of his kicking at the wooden slats.

By the time he opened the stall and peered in, the animal had calmed down. As much as Storm ever calmed down.

The horse stopped, but blew through his nostrils as he tapped his hoof on the straw floor, then he danced backward. Finally the ritual stopped, but those midnight-black eyes still regarded Johnny with suspicion.

Johnny didn't break eye contact with the huge animal. A good sixteen hands high with a black glistening coat, Night Storm was an impressive stallion. And he could be dangerous. That he had to remember first and foremost.

The horse rushed forward, trying to frighten him off, but Johnny quickly raised his hands and waved Storm back. Spooked, the animal reared up. Johnny stood his ground and opened the bottom half of the door. Speaking softly, Johnny moved slowly and managed to attach a long lead rope. He slowly walked him out of the stall.

Everyone knew to stay back when the horse was in transit. Outside, Wes was standing away from the pen, but motioned with a thumbs-up.

Johnny nodded and got the horse into the pen and let him run.

Wes walked over. "Good job."

"All in a day's work," Johnny told him, still watching Storm. "Seems easier than answering questions from Brady."

Wes laughed. "The boy does have the gift of gab."

Johnny had never spent much time with kids. He'd avoided it. They came with baggage and were needy and wanted all your attention. All right, Brady talked a lot, but he was polite and his favorite topic was his grandfather. And even he had liked the stories about Clay Calhoun. The kid looked up to his grandfather, and his respect seemed to have been well earned.

Johnny thought back to his own childhood. Not a good one. Talk about baggage. He'd been about fourteen when he'd run away from his mother and her abusive boyfriend. But there had been some good moments, too. Will Nichols stood out as the one man he'd respected and cared about the most. Will had found him hiding out in his barn, but instead of calling the law or making him go back, the old man had offered him a place to stay whenever he needed it.

Johnny hadn't stayed long. He decided he'd search for his biological father, thinking the man would be happy to meet his son. All he knew about Jake Jameson was that he was a musician, traveling around to honky-tonks and bars with his band.

In the end, he never caught up to his father. He finally gave up and went back to Will's place. The old horse trainer had been the closest thing to home and family Johnny had ever had. Will also taught him everything about training horses.

"Need any help?" Wes asked as they watched Storm charge around.

"Maybe you could hang around to see if this pen holds up."

Wes walked closer. "Wouldn't mind that at all."

Johnny went into the pen and picked up the lead rope and started the horse moving around in a tight circle. If nothing else was accomplished, Storm would get some exercise.

Jess pulled up at the ranch at about four o'clock. She started toward the house, but stopped when she saw some of the men standing at the corral.

Curious, she headed toward the barn, then around to the metal pen that had been constructed by Wes and the ranch hands for Storm's training.

She stopped when she saw the stallion circling the arena. Storm looked a lot calmer.

As she got closer, Johnny snapped the end of the long lead rope against the ground. Dust scattered and Storm gave a high-pitched whinny, but with ears pinned back, the animal did as commanded and changed his direction.

Jess looked at Johnny. He stood tall and lean with

wide shoulders that carried off the cowboy look—
Western shirt, faded jeans and boots. But this man
looked better than most. Sure and confident, Johnny
moved around animals as if he were born to it. No
doubt, he had a special gift. She was sure her father
had seen that same talent.

Looking at the setting sun, she realized they were
losing daylight. In the winter months the days were
much shorter. The training ended as Johnny opened the
gate and walked out leading a resistant horse back to
the barn. She followed from a safe distance, and once
he closed the stall gate, she walked over.

He turned just as she arrived. She wasn't dressed
for a walk in the barn. Her heels made maneuvering
difficult.

"Checking on my progress?"

"Not really. I was checking to see if Brady should
see any of this. I think he should keep away for now—
Storm seems calmer but his behavior is still question-
able at best."

"I agree, Brady doesn't need to be around the horse
right now. Not with his fears. So I'll be the bad guy
and tell him."

She opened her mouth to argue, and stopped. "I'm
still baffled as to why my son, who's always been afraid
of horses since that incident with my dad, wants to see
this out-of-control stallion."

"I believe it's because Storm is your dad's horse."

In her high heels, Jess walked gingerly down the
aisle. "I guess that could be it."

Seeing her difficulty, Johnny took her by the elbow
to help her maneuver out of the barn to the gravel com-

pound area that led to the house. There was a warm strength in his touch. He made her feel small and feminine. Whoa. She didn't need this right now. Now? No, never. No more cowboys.

"What do you know about Storm's history?" he asked as they approached the split-rail fence that surrounded the ranch house. "Did you know the previous owner?"

"There are records. Probably in Dad's—I mean, Holt's office."

"Have you been around the horse much?"

She shrugged. "I was there with Dad the day he bought him. He'd seen a picture of Storm on the internet." She looked up at him in the dimming sunlight. His gray eyes got her attention again. How could you not stare at them? His dark skin and long black lashes made them stand out.

"It was a horse ranch outside San Antonio," she told him. "I still remember seeing him that first time. Big and muscular, he had nearly perfect proportions. Dad was taken, too. It was love at first sight."

She turned back to Johnny and found him staring at her. "Do you believe in love at first sight, Jess?" he asked in a husky voice.

His words sent a warm shiver through her. All at once she caught her heel in the gravel and lost her balance. "Oh," she cried as she started to go down, then she felt Johnny's arms come around her and pull her upright. She ended up against his solid chest.

"You okay?" he asked.

She nodded and he set her back on her feet. "I shouldn't have come out with these shoes."

She caught his grin. "Oh, I don't know. Then I wouldn't have gotten to see your gorgeous legs."

Heat rose to her cheeks and she wasn't sure what to say to that. Then she heard the back door open and her son called her name.

She moved away from Johnny to see Brady running toward them. Jess took several steps back from the man. "Hi, honey." She hugged her child, then zipped up his jacket to ward off the chill.

Brady went to Johnny. "Did Storm do better this time?"

Johnny crouched down to the boy's height. "Hey, buddy," he said. "We talked about this. Storm has a long way to go before he's safe."

"But you're gonna fix him, right?"

"I'm going to try my best. That's why I don't want anyone around to bother Storm while we're working."

The boy sighed. "Okay, I won't bother him. But when he starts behaving can I see him?"

Jess watched a smile appear on Johnny's face. He was good to her son and she appreciated that. "I'll come and get you myself."

"Will you tell me how you train him?" Brady asked.

"Sure. Anytime."

The boy turned to his mother. "Mom, can Johnny come to supper tonight? 'Cause we have to talk about stuff."

Great. "Well, I don't know, maybe Johnny has plans for tonight."

The man grinned. "My social calendar just happens to be clear." He took Brady's hand and the two walked hand in hand toward the house.

Jess had planned to go back to her place and fix supper there, but hearing the sweet laughter coming from her son, she decided she could put up with the good-looking Johnny Jameson for a few hours.

CHAPTER FOUR

LATER at the ranch house, the fireplace was lit and the kitchen had a warm and cozy feel. Johnny didn't do warm and cozy, recalling his past attempts at it. Not with his kind of life.

Then he glanced at Jess and felt a stirring in his gut. Damn, he wanted her. This wasn't good. He thought about Molly and the time he'd spent with her today. She was a pretty woman and he liked her well enough. She was more his type. Yeah, he needed to stay where it was safe. No strings. No kids. But the problem was, he was attracted to Jess.

"Johnny, how many horses have you talked to?" Brady asked.

Johnny bit back a smile. The kid's big brown eyes were darker than his mother's, but just as expressive. "I guess I never thought about counting them."

"We can start now. Your horse, Risky, is one. And Storm is two." Brady frowned. "Do you remember any more? We should write them down on paper. I can't do it, I only know how to write my name."

"Brady," his mother began. "How about we save that for another day? I got that new video today you've been asking for."

The boy started to argue, then thought better of it. "Okay." He climbed down and his mother took him into the other room.

When Jess finally came back she refilled their coffee cups.

He smiled. "Thank you."

"You're welcome."

"Oh, Jess," Johnny began. "I meant to ask, how'd your meeting go with the grocery chain?"

"Not too bad." She smiled. "We'll have limited shelf space to start, but I get five stores."

"I take it that's good," Johnny cheered.

Earlier in the day Molly had told Johnny about Jess's beginnings. How she'd started up her bakery pretty much on her own. With an inheritance from her mother and a cosigned loan from her father, Jess began selling Sandra's Preserves and then her baked goods. And all while she was raising her baby.

Once again, Johnny wondered about Brady's father. The man had to be out of his mind to leave this woman. He took a sip of his coffee. Most guys would trip over themselves to get a chance to be with her.

From what little he'd learned about Jess, she'd pretty much kept to herself and her family. Maybe it was time he helped change that.

"Jess, do you dance?"

She blinked. "What?"

He smiled. "I heard about this dance being held at the Cattleman's Hall. It's this weekend."

"Who told you? Wes?"

"I first heard about it at the gas station from Gus."

Jess smiled. "That man can talk your arm off."

Johnny shrugged. "He seems harmless."

"He's a wonderful man, and was a good friend of my dad. They went to school together. And he's come to my rescue a few times."

Johnny caught her sad look. He expected being a single mother in a small town hadn't been easy for her. Of course, there was no doubt that Clay Calhoun had protected his daughter. Was that the reason Jess stayed to herself? Were people cruel to her?

Well, it had better not happen when he was around. "I was wondering, since I'm new in town…would you like to go to the dance?"

"What?"

"I asked if you would like to go to the dance this coming weekend."

Jess froze. She hadn't been asked out in a while. Most men left her alone. She gave them plenty of reasons to stay away. "I can't… I don't go out."

"Is it me, or just every man?"

She felt the rush of excitement from Johnny's attention, but she was also frightened by it. Before she could answer, a child's cries filled the room and she took off for the family room with Johnny close behind her.

Jess quickly reached for the boy on the sofa and began soothing his fears. "Aw, honey. Did you have a bad dream?"

The boy buried his head against his mother and nodded. "It scared me."

"Well, you're okay now."

Brady looked up and saw Johnny.

"Hey, there, partner." He was drawn to the boy, wanting to help. "Rough dream?"

"Yeah, it was about Storm. He hurt you."

Johnny knelt down beside mother and son. "Hey, that's not going to happen. I'm very careful. And I'm good at my job." He touched the boy's mussed hair. "That's the reason I don't let anybody too close when I work him. Storm gets nervous, too." He felt Jess's nearness. "If you're there, then I'll worry."

"Kinda like when Mom worries about me and she wants to hold my hand."

"Yeah, like that."

The boy yawned.

Jess straightened. "It's time for you to go to bed."

Brady started to argue and Johnny said, "How about if I give you a piggyback ride?"

Those were magic words for the kid. "Wow!"

If there was any protest from Jess, he didn't hear it.

He turned around so Brady could climb on his back. Once he felt the tiny arms go around his neck, something tightened in his chest. He grabbed hold of his legs, and asked, "Ready?"

"Yeah."

Johnny stood, saying, "Tell me where to go."

Johnny knew that even though Jess and Brady lived in an apartment on the west side of the ranch land, sometimes they would stay over in the main ranch house. Brady showed Johnny the way and he carried the boy into the hall to a winding staircase with a hand-carved banister. He climbed the carpeted steps to the second floor where there were several family pictures along the wall. They slowed as Brady pointed out the one of Clay Calhoun. The big, barrel-chested rancher had a ready smile as he stood alongside his wife and his two sons and two daughters. A very young Brady was held in his arms.

A perfect family.

"That was before Grandma Sandy went to heaven," Brady told him. "I was little when she died."

"It's nice to have this photo to look at."

They continued down a long hall past several bedrooms, and Johnny wondered what it would have been like to grow up here. It was so different from his idea of a family. Just another reason to keep his distance from Clay's daughter.

Finally they came to a room that was painted blue and had a single bed covered with a plaid comforter.

"End of the line, kid." He let the boy bounce onto the bed and was rewarded by giggles. Johnny turned and noticed Brady's mother didn't look amused by the antics. She stripped the boy of his jeans and shirt, then made quick work of putting on his pajamas.

Johnny stepped back as she put the boy under the blanket. "I better hit the hay, too."

"No!" the child cried.

"Brady, you can't keep taking up all of Johnny's time. He has to get up early tomorrow."

The boy relented. "Sorry, but I gotta ask him something."

"It's all right," Johnny answered.

Jess stepped back. She didn't understand any of this. Her son didn't usually act like this with strangers. "All right, young man, what's going on?"

Brady looked up at Johnny.

"You better come clean, kid."

"Papa Clay talked a lot about Storm. He didn't want anyone to hurt him ever again."

"Honey, Johnny isn't going to hurt Storm. He doesn't hurt horses. Uncle Holt wouldn't allow it."

"I know. That's why I want Johnny to help me not be afraid of horses so I can help take care of Storm forever."

Jess caught a smile starting on Johnny's mouth.

"Brady, that's a good idea. But Storm isn't a happy horse right now. Maybe you should hang out with a pony or a yearling first. So you'll get used to animals."

The child nodded. "So you will help me learn to ride a horse?"

"Brady Clayton Calhoun," Jess said, having had enough of this. "This is something you and I need to talk about before any decision is made."

"But you're too busy and Uncle Holt is gone. Papa said Johnny's the best. So he needs to do it."

Jess pulled back the covers and tucked her son into the bed. "We'll talk about this later."

"But, Mom…"

She kissed him. "Brady, go to sleep."

He hugged his mother. "Night, Johnny."

"Night, partner."

Johnny walked out and Jess was close behind. She hit the light and closed the door. "I am so sorry my son put you on the spot. I don't expect you to do any of this."

Jess could see his hesitation. "I can start the lessons," he told her. "I'm just not sure if I'll be around long enough to follow through with as much help as the boy needs." Johnny's gaze went to hers. "It's up to you if you feel it's not a good idea."

She released a long breath. She didn't know what to do. "You know Brady's fears. I can't deny that my dad was hoping one day he would feel differently."

They were standing in the dim hall now.

"Like I said, it's your decision."

She couldn't let this get personal with how she felt about Johnny. "I insist on paying you for helping Brady."

He shook his head. "You pay me very well for training Storm." His face broke into a grin. "But we can barter with something else."

She felt her entire body grow warm. "I'm afraid to ask."

He moved close, and she fought to stand her ground. "Nothing bad, Ms. Calhoun. It's just that since you won't be my date, maybe you could at least save me a few dances."

Funny. Jess wasn't sure if she was happy or disappointed with his demand.

Although Jess had always been an early riser, she had trouble getting out of bed the next morning. With coffee in hand, she headed to the one bathroom in her two-bedroom apartment.

Reaching into the large shower stall she turned on the water and hoped that it would help revive her.

Fifteen minutes later, she had finished blow-drying her hair, then wove the blond strands into her standard single braid. After adding a little makeup and lip gloss, she slipped on her dark trousers and a white polo shirt with the embroidered Jess's Bakery over the pocket.

Next year her morning ritual would be easier. Brady would start kindergarten and the school bus would pick him up practically at the bakery door. Until then, she still had to work out a schedule with Nancy. The house-keeper liked watching Brady, but Jess didn't like to impose, even though Nancy's time had freed up since Dad's passing, and especially with Holt out of town.

She left her bedroom and walked down the hall to the living/kitchen area. It wasn't the largest space, but big enough for her and Brady.

For now.

But since the death of her dad, she was beginning to realize how much her son needed a man in his life. And she admitted that she did, too. Maybe someday she would that find that special guy to build a future with. To find a father for Brady. Her thoughts turned to Johnny.

Oh, no. Sorry, no matter how good-looking, he wasn't the guy for her. He wasn't the stay-around kind. And she needed that kind of man.

Jess grabbed her jacket and purse, then walked out the door. She jogged down the steps and circled around the side of the building to the bakery's kitchen door. Stepping inside, she stopped and looked around.

Stainless-steel appliances and countertops filled the spacious area. She was surprised to see that the day's work had begun. Round pans were lined on the counter as the carrot cake ingredients were being poured into each one by part-time baker Maria Cruz.

Jess greeted her as she opened the large convection oven and helped transfer the cake pans inside.

Once completed, she set the timer and Maria went to mix up the chocolate batter.

She greeted Carol Dayton. "I didn't realize I was late getting here." She glanced at the clock; it wasn't even five-thirty. "Why the early start?"

"We got an order for three dozen loaves of bread for the women's club luncheon today in San Marcos. It came in yesterday while you were at your meeting."

Jess groaned. "San Marcos? That's far away."

Carol uncovered the fresh dough from under the towel and fed it into a kneading machine. "It's not a problem, and they're paying extra for delivery."

Nothing ever seemed to rattle Carol Dayton. Jess looked at the woman with her ready smile and pretty green eyes. She wore her once wheat-colored hair, now streaked with gray, in a bun at the back of her head. She and her husband, Ben, had lost a lot, including their ranch. They never felt sorry for themselves, just moved on, together. It was a blessing for Jess. They worked for her now, and practically ran the business. They'd been like a second set of parents. She didn't know what she would do without either one of them.

Jess grabbed a clean apron from the drawer and tied it around her waist, then went to wash her hands in the deep sink. She wasn't the main baker any longer. Sometimes it bothered her that she wasn't able to always put her special touch on every one of the items that left the store.

All the recipes were hers and her mother's. The carrot cake, the double Dutch chocolate cake, the Russian loaf, along with the pies. The custard cream was her special recipe. She'd only shared the recipes with the Dayton family.

After drying her hands, Jess went to the other side of the counter to help Carol. She began transferring the bread dough from the machine and twisting it into shape on the baking sheet. She glanced around to see that they were missing someone.

"Where's Molly?"

"She's out in the warehouse with Ben. She'll be here in time to frost the cakes."

Molly was the artist at the bakery. She did all the decorating of the cakes.

"I could call her if you need her."

"No, that's okay."

Jess had been surprised by her friend's disappearance yesterday afternoon. It wasn't like Molly not even to call about the meeting. And when she called her later, she got her voice mail. A few minutes later, her friend sent her a text, telling her to go for it.

No doubt her friend had ideas that Jess was interested in Johnny Jameson, and was suggesting she act on it.

The back door opened and Molly walked in.

"Hi," Jess said.

"Hi."

She didn't like the way that sounded. "Molly, could I talk with you?"

"Sure. How did things turn out with Johnny last night?"

Jess took her friend into the front of the store. "What

are you talking about? I wanted to see you when I got back from the meeting. Nancy said you left early."

Molly smiled. "All Johnny talked about was you." She shrugged. "I didn't want to hang around to see you get cozy with him."

"We didn't get cozy. We had supper and talked about his work on Dad's horse, Storm."

"Look, Jess. I got the message at lunch. Anyone could see the man is interested in you. I thought if I left quietly things might happen. You didn't need me around."

Jess didn't want to think about the attraction she felt for the man. "I didn't do anything to encourage him."

"It didn't change the fact that he couldn't take his eyes off you at lunch. Come on, Jess." Her friend gave her an incredulous look. "You have to be blind not to see it."

Maybe I don't want to see it. "What does it matter? I don't go for cowboys."

Molly laughed. "Now I know you're crazy. The man is to die for."

She shook her head. "He's a wanderer, Mol. He told me himself that he practically lives out of his trailer. He won't be here much past a few weeks, maybe a month. He travels light—his truck, trailer and a duffel bag. That's it. And even if I was interested, which I'm not," she stressed, hating that she was fibbing to her friend, "I have far too many strings tying me here."

"Maybe you'll be the one who changes the man and he'll stay."

Jess raised her arms and let them drop. "You know how good I am at getting men to stick around."

"One man," Molly stressed. "Chad was bad news from the start. That doesn't mean all men are."

She didn't want to do this. "I have Brady to think about. He's my first concern always and he could be hurt if I get involved with someone and he leaves. Brady's still recovering from his grandfather's death."

"I can understand that. It's just you've buried yourself in this business. There are so many nice guys in town that would like it if you'd give them the time of day. What's wrong with Drew Sanders? He owns the Lone Star Mercantile so I'd say he's got a stable income. He's not a wanderer, because his family has lived around here for a few generations."

"He's nice enough," Jess said, but she knew there were no sparks with Drew.

"Not bad-looking, either," Molly added. "And he's asked you out...how many times?"

"I've been a little busy with Brady and the business."

"Jess, you still need to take time for yourself. You need time to play with grown-ups."

Jess couldn't help but think about Johnny and his invitation. "I don't know if I want to date right now."

"I understand. You're a little rusty. So how about a girls' night out? You, me, Nancy. Oh, oh, I know just the thing. We'll go to the Cattleman's Hall dance this Saturday."

Panic nearly choked her. "I can't. I don't have a babysitter."

"I'll watch Brady."

Molly and Jess swung around to see Carol in the doorway. "In fact, he can spend the night if you want."

Brady loved the Dayton family. "Oh, Carol, I can't ask you to give up your weekend."

The older woman came to her. "You didn't ask, I offered. We love Brady as if he were ours."

Jess was touched. "Thank you. We'll probably make an early night of it."

"Not if I can help it," Molly added. "Thanks, Mom."

"Don't thank me yet. I'm hoping Jess will be a good influence on you and keep you in line."

Jess grinned. "Now you are asking the impossible."

CHAPTER FIVE

SATURDAY night came too soon for Jess.

She drew an encouraging breath as she walked into the Cattleman's Association Hall. After changing her outfit three times, she had finally decided on a denim skirt, a Western-cut pink blouse and chain belt. Her hand-tooled boots were the pair her father had bought her for her past birthday. With Molly's prodding, she nixed her usual braid and left her hair free in natural curls.

She glanced at her friend. Molly wore her black jeans and fitted blouse tucked into a wide belt with a Western buckle. Oh, yeah, she was clearly looking for a man.

Nancy was in a skirt also, and looked pretty with her hair down in soft waves. She smiled as she glanced around the crowded room, trying not to be obvious as she searched for her guy.

Wes suddenly appeared at Nancy's side. He greeted all of them, then took his girl off to dance.

Molly nodded toward the couple moving to the sultry ballad. "Those two should get married."

Jess knew little of Nancy's past, only that she'd gone

through a rough divorce before she came to the ranch ten years ago. "Maybe they aren't ready."

"But sneaking around can get old."

Jess recalled a couple of times in the past few months when she had arrived early and discovered Wes leaving Nancy's room off the kitchen. "It's called being discreet."

"If they get any closer, everyone's going to know how they feel."

They both broke into laughter, but soon one of the local ranch hands came by and escorted Molly to the dance floor. This was what Jess had always hated, standing around on her own, feeling anxious. She wanted to dance, but at the same time, she didn't. Would Johnny come tonight? Would he dance with her?

No, she didn't need to think about him.

Then one of her dad's friends, Charlie Powers, came by. "You're too pretty to be standing by yourself," he began as he took her out to dance. "Are the men around here crazy?"

"I might be putting them off," she admitted.

"It's good to be picky. You should expect nothing but the best, Jess Calhoun." The older man smiled. "You let me know if any of them give you any trouble, you hear?"

"Thank you, Charlie." The music stopped and she kissed his cheek. "Now, go dance with that pretty wife of yours." She shoved him off toward Sally and went in the other direction to get off the floor as the band started to play a George Strait song. But before she reached her destination, someone took hold of her arm. She turned around and found Johnny.

He grinned, slow and wicked. "I believe this is our dance?"

She found herself nodding and he pulled her into an embrace and began the two-step. She was surprised that she was able to follow his lead. It'd been years since she danced with a man. A man she'd cared about. No. No, she couldn't care about Johnny.

Yet, she couldn't dismiss what it felt like to have this man hold her. He set her off in a series of spins and managed to maneuver her back into his arms.

"You're a pretty good dancer," she told him.

"Had some practice."

Her heart was racing as she concentrated on the steps. Of course a man like Johnny Jameson would have been out with a lot of women, too. Question was, should she be one of them?

Finally the music ended, but the band went right into the next song. This time it was a Garth Brooks ballad. Johnny drew her close, his eyes already mesmerizing her.

His arm tightened around her waist, drawing her against him as his breath caressed her cheek. His thighs brushed hers and she felt a shiver run down her spine. Oh, boy, she was headed for trouble. Problem was, she didn't care. She liked the feelings this man stirred in her. What would it hurt for one evening?

"Having fun?" she asked.

"Holding a pretty woman in my arms? Oh, yeah."

She sucked in a breath. "I meant, are you meeting people?"

"I've met enough. I'd rather concentrate on the woman I'm holding right now." He pulled her close again and rested his chin against her forehead. Her breasts pressed to his chest. She heard his low groan and he pulled back.

"Come on." He took her hand and moved through the crowd until they reached a patio area. There were heat lamps to ward off the cold and ashtrays for the smokers. He kept walking until they reached a dark corner. He turned her around.

"Johnny. Is something wrong?"

"You can't be that naive, Jess." Johnny studied her in the dim light. When he'd spotted her tonight, he'd planned to stay away, but she drew him like a magnet. Definitely, Jess Calhoun was trouble and he was crazy to mess with her—but she was too hard to resist.

He leaned down and lightly brushed his lips across hers once, then again, only allowing him a small taste of her. He fought for control as she pressed her body against his, eager to deepen the kiss, and finally pulled back. Pressing his forehead against hers, he waited for his heart rate to slow to normal. "You're playing with fire."

She looked up at him with innocent eyes.

"Okay, that's it. You're coming with me."

"Where are you taking me this time?"

"Hopefully to safer ground."

Jess wasn't sure if she was disappointed or not. They ended up sitting in a booth at Gracie May's. Since everyone was at the dance, the place was nearly deserted. Yet, she enjoyed being with Johnny. Alone. Even knowing that it was a bad idea, just a sample of his kiss had her aching for more.

He ordered them coffee and a piece of carrot cake.

"You left the dance because you were suddenly hungry?"

He leaned closer. "When you press your body against a man, you send messages to him. The wrong messages."

She fought the blush, but failed. "You kissed me."

"Because you're so damn tempting."

Really? She looked tempting? It had been so long since she let a man get close. She found she enjoyed Johnny's attention. Her hands cupped her mug, trying to act as if she heard those words all the time. Yet, she also felt the ache inside knowing how much she wanted to hear them…from this man.

Johnny sat back when the waitress, Bonnie, brought the cake. He thanked her. "This isn't a good idea, Jess. You have to know that I don't do anything permanent, and I doubt you do one-night stands."

She glanced away. "No, I don't. And I wasn't looking for one tonight. You asked me to the dance but I decided to go with Molly and Nancy. It's not like I tracked you down and threw myself at you."

Johnny couldn't help but wonder if she knew how men reacted to her. He'd watched several guys eyeing her. He told himself that he only asked her to dance to protect her. But hell, he was worse. She needed to be protected from him.

"Just so you know, I don't usually go out much. I mean, I became a mother at an early age, so I've pretty much stayed close to home."

Johnny wasn't surprised. "Who was this fool who left you high and dry?"

She looked surprised at his bold question. "Just a young cowboy passing through who worked at the ranch. I'd come home from college for the summer and Chad and I got together. Old story—I fell in love and was devastated when he took off after I told him I was pregnant. He made it clear he didn't want me or the baby."

Johnny cursed.

She realized she couldn't stop. She wanted it all out in the open. "After Brady was born, Dad tracked Chad down but only to have him sign away any parental rights." She looked Johnny in the eye. "He signed it. There was probably some money involved, but I know what my dad did was out of love." She blinked several times. "Now Clay's gone, and Brady and I are having a bit of a rough patch, especially with the rest of my family away."

Johnny felt his heart pounding. He wanted to find this Chad character and pound some sense into him. Instead, he remained calm.

"I shouldn't have dragged you away from the dance, Jess. I was out of line."

She smiled. "I'm kind of glad you did. The hall was crowded and the music too loud. Oh, maybe you want to go back."

He shook his head. "I'm happy right where I am." He picked up the fork, cut a piece of cake and took a bite.

The combination of flavors burst in his mouth. "Damn, this is good." He dug in for another sample. "You made this?"

Smiling, she nodded. "As you can see I'm more than a pretty face."

He took another helping. "Now that's something we both agree on."

An hour later and after a second piece of cake, Johnny walked Jess back to the dance. She met up with her friends and they invited her and Johnny to go with them to the Saddle Up Bar and Grill.

Jess had declined and so did Johnny. Since she'd brought her car, she decided to drive home. That was when Johnny said he'd follow her. A thrill rushed through her thinking about Johnny coming up to her apartment. Would she invite him in? Was she ready for more than some harmless flirting, and a whisper of a kiss? The problem was resolved when he climbed out of his truck and asked to see her bakery.

She unlocked the back door to the kitchen, turned off the alarm, then flipped on the under-counter lighting, leaving the room in a soft glow. She stepped back and left Johnny to do his own inspection.

He removed his hat and went right to the heart of her work area, and ran his hand along the stainless-steel counter. She noticed his long tapered fingers. She shivered recalling those same hands touching her, holding her close.

"Jess?"

"Sorry. What?"

He leaned against the counter, his arms folded over his chest. "This is really something. How long have you been here?"

"It was built about two years ago. My mail-order

business for Sandra's Preserves had taken over the ranch kitchen so I needed to move. It only made sense to add the ovens in the kitchen design along with the storefront.

"My dad loved my desserts and he convinced me to dream big. So I started with a few cakes and pies to offer to the store walk-ins. They sold out quickly. Then Gracie May's asked to order my baked goods on a daily basis."

She shrugged. "Word got out, and I hired some help. I couldn't do any of this without Molly, and her parents. Carol runs this kitchen, and Ben does all the mail orders for the preserves. Since this building is on Calhoun property, I can expand even more. Maybe add on a sandwich shop next door." She walked to the doorway at the front of the store. "We can cut a hole in the wall and add a deli. I'm not the only good cook here. Molly's mother makes the best potato salad and coleslaw."

She caught Johnny's grin, slow and easy.

"What?"

"Nothing, I just enjoy listening to you. I bet you have more big plans?"

She liked that he was eager to listen. "As a matter of fact, yes, I do. I want to add several other buildings. Downtown Larkville doesn't have many specialty shops. Not enough to bring people off the highway to spend money." She waved her hand. "But that's far off in the future. Maybe when Brady's in school all day."

Johnny knew some people had their entire lives mapped out. A home, business…family. He thought back to his past. The hurt and tears he'd caused someone he'd truly cared about because he didn't want to settle down. A lonely ache gripped his chest.

"What about you, Johnny Jameson? Do you think you'll ever put down roots, and let people bring their horses to you?"

He shook his head. "It's easier to go to the problem horse. And I can charge extra for travel. Besides, I like going to different parts of the country."

"Where do you come from?"

He shrugged. "That's a little hard to answer. My mom moved around a lot. I'm not really sure where she had me. She said it was a small town in the Texas panhandle, around Amarillo."

Jess gave him a puzzled look. "Is your mother still alive?"

"Can't honestly answer that, either," he said, thinking about the mean lowlife who'd beat her. "We parted company a long time ago."

She went to him. "Ah, Johnny. I'm sorry."

He tensed when her hand touched his arm. He was feeling too raw, and it would be so easy to take her comfort. "Don't be. It was a long time ago. I haven't been that kid for a long time."

Her deep gaze had him wondering what it would be like to get lost in her.

"What about your dad?" she asked.

"You're just full of questions tonight."

"Just getting to know you," she offered.

He started to protest, then relented. "Seems old Jake never wanted to be found. Not by his son, anyway." Why was he suddenly spilling his guts? "Hey, sometimes it's better to cut bait and move on." He looked at her. "In my family we're not like the Calhouns—we never put down roots."

"Maybe you should think about it." She moved in closer, giving him a look that could only mean trouble. For him. "Larkville is a nice place to settle down." She placed her hand on his chest. "You could probably do well for yourself."

He laid his hand over hers, but didn't move it right away. Did she feel his pounding heart? Did she know she caused it?

He finally stepped away. At the sound of his name on her lips, he turned back to her. He needed to do something to scare her off. To let her know that he could hurt her.

Yet, when he saw that combination of innocence and desire in her eyes, he cupped her face in his hands, bent down and kissed her. No soft brush this time, he captured her mouth with all the hunger Jess Calhoun had caused in him since he'd first laid eyes on her.

Catching her gasp, he pressed his tongue into her sweet mouth. Her hands went to his chest and he felt the heat through his shirt. Finally her arms circled his neck and she opened her mouth so he could deepen the kiss.

By the time he pulled away, he was dizzy, but quickly coming to his senses. "Damn, woman. I think I better get out of here before I get us both into trouble."

When Jess started to speak, he placed a finger against those well-kissed lips. "Good night, Jess."

Johnny had slept like hell, and it showed during the morning workout with Storm. He'd had trouble keeping the stallion focused on his task. Okay, he knew he could expect to have bad days. That didn't mean he had to like it, especially when he knew it'd been his fault for letting Jess Calhoun get to him. For letting her occupy his thoughts when he had a job to do.

It was hard not to think about the kisses they'd shared last night. Thank God he'd been smart enough to stop things with Jess when he had, or he might have ended up with an awkward morning with his boss. He closed his eyes. He didn't need the complication.

He stepped out of the corral to give the stallion and himself a break.

Wes came up to him. "Someone is trying to get your attention."

Johnny glanced toward the house and saw Brady waving at him. He waved back. He also caught sight of Jess on the porch. She was in the distance, but he could see she was dressed in hip-hugging jeans and boots today. Not that she didn't look good in them, but he'd also enjoyed seeing those gorgeous legs of hers at the dance.

"Jess seemed to have a good time at the dance last night," Wes commented.

"Yeah, I guess she did." He placed a hand on the metal railing, aware of the horse pacing in the arena behind him. "We both did," Johnny said. When he saw Jess heading toward them, he felt a stirring inside.

She hugged her heavy jacket around her against the winter cold.

"Hey, Jess," Johnny greeted her.

"Hi, Wes. Johnny. I don't want to disturb either of you, but if you have a minute…"

"Sure," Wes said.

"Not a problem, Storm's working off some frustration."

That brought a smile to her pretty mouth, reminding him of how good she'd tasted last night.

He shook away the direction of his thoughts. "What do you need?"

"Brady has been talking nonstop about learning to ride. So I'm taking your advice, Johnny, and starting Brady out with a pony."

"Well, I'll be damned." Wes grinned. "Clay would have loved that."

She turned toward the foreman. "Wes, Brady's birthday is at the end of the month. Do you think you could find Brady a pony?"

"Great idea." The foreman took off his hat, and ran a hand over his short hair. "The Carson Ranch has a couple. Do you think Brady would like to pick it out himself?"

Jess smiled and Johnny felt a tightening in his gut. "What do you think?"

Wes laughed. "He is a lot like his grandfather in that respect. Likes to make his own decisions. I'll go give Carson a call and let you know." The foreman left them and headed toward the barn.

Johnny watched as emotions played across Jess's face. "My dad would have loved taking Brady for his first ride."

He wished the man was here for her, too. "Hey, your daddy will always be with the boy," Johnny said. "And doesn't Brady have great memories of him and Clay together?"

"I'm sorry. Brady's been lucky. You hadn't even gotten the chance to meet your father."

Jess watched him shrug as if it didn't matter. Oh, it mattered all right, even more than he let on. She was beginning to see there was more to this man than his way with horses. More to the reason he'd been going from place to place trying to fit somewhere.

"It's okay. Some men aren't cut out to be fathers. He was lucky to have Clay to teach him the things that are important in life. Like love and respect, being truthful."

"You're right." She sighed, then turned to him. "Johnny, Brady would love to start those riding lessons you talked about. If you're available, of course I'll pay for your time."

Johnny shook his head. "I won't take payment for something I promised the boy."

"But—"

"No, I won't take any more of your money."

Jess didn't know what it was about this man. He was so different than what she'd expected when she first met him. From the way he made her feel, to how he treated her son. She nodded. "My son can be a handful," she told him. "And he still might never get on a horse."

"Oh, you might be surprised." He smiled at her and there was that flutter in her stomach again. "From what I've seen so far, he's a Calhoun through and through."

"It's you, Johnny. You challenge him to do things. I guess I treat him like a baby still."

"You're excused because you're his mother."

There were so many things she hadn't been able to give him. "I should be teaching him how to be independent, too."

"He'll get there." Johnny leaned closer. "Look how he's fighting everyone about riding. That's why I want to help him. He's ready, Jess. Let him prove himself."

For the first time in a long time she trusted another man outside of her family. "Okay, I agree. Would you like to come for supper and we can tell him the news?"

Considering what happened between them last night, Johnny wondered if he should keep his distance. "You don't need to feed me all the time."

"I know, but you're doing a big favor for me."

Behind them, Storm gave an impatient whinny and he knew that restless feeling when it came to this woman. "Well, if you're guaranteeing dessert, of course I'll be there."

"Do you have a favorite?"

Johnny tried not to react. "Surprise me."

"Okay, your Dutch apple pie is my new favorite." Johnny pushed aside his empty plate and leaned back in the chair.

Jess couldn't help but be pleased the man liked her cooking. "It was my dad's favorite, too."

"It's mine, too," Brady said, making sure they didn't forget that he was at the table.

"Every dessert is your favorite," Nancy said as she cleared away the dishes and brought back the coffee-pot and refilled their mugs.

"I don't like coconut cream pie." The boy made a face. "It's icky."

"You make coconut cream pie?" Johnny asked Jess. She nodded.

"Man, between Nancy's cooking, and these desserts, I may never leave the Double Bar C."

"Good." Brady's face lit up. "You can train all the horses at the ranch. Can't he, Mom?"

Jess couldn't stop her son's hero worship, even if she tried. "I bet he could," she agreed, but knew he would have other jobs to go to somewhere else. Why did it matter to her that he had to leave?

Johnny took a sip of his coffee. "First of all, I need to help Storm. And I hear that a little boy needs to learn how to ride."

Brady grinned. "That's me."

"You sure about this?" Wes asked.

The child nodded. "Yes. I'm almost five. A lot of the kids in my school know how and Tucker Carson has a pony. Topper."

Jess couldn't believe she was saying this. "So do you think you'd like a pony for your birthday?"

Brady's brown eyes widened. "Oh, boy. Can I?"

She nodded. "Wes can take us to find one you like."

"Yeah. Can Johnny go, too?"

Johnny jumped in. "Sure, I'd like that."

Brady gave a fist pump. "It's gonna be the best birthday ever."

Jess's heart swelled, seeing her son so happy. She looked at Johnny, knowing he was one of the reasons. She wasn't sure if that was good news or bad news. When his job was finished he'd move on. Where would that leave her and her son?

CHAPTER SIX

LATER that night, Johnny pulled up next to the small SUV beside the bakery and went up the steps leading to the second-story apartment and Jess's home.

It was nearly ten o'clock. He was usually headed for bed, planning his morning schedule, but he couldn't leave things without talking to Jess. He was becoming too involved with both mother and son. And he'd feel better setting some ground rules.

He rapped on the door before he could change his mind. He waited, then heard a muffled, "Who's there?"

"Johnny."

The lock gave way and the door swung open. Jess appeared in her same clothes as earlier. Good, he hadn't woken her up. "Johnny, what are you doing here?"

"We need to talk."

She hesitated, then opened the door to let him inside. He removed his hat and looked around the room. It was surprisingly large with a sectional sofa that faced a flat-screen television. The lighting was dim, except for the lamp at the desk in the corner. Soft music played in the background. He turned toward the small but open kitchen, next to a narrow hall that probably led to the bedrooms.

"Is something wrong?" she asked, drawing his attention back.

He turned around and saw those whiskey-colored eyes looking back at him. Hell, she was killing him. "I could lie and say I came to talk about teaching Brady."

"You changed your mind?" she asked, then rushed on to say, "I understand. I mean, he's a little boy and it's not going to be an easy job."

"Dammit, Jess, it's not that. I like your son. I wanted to talk about what happened between us." He paced the small room. "I mean, there's an attraction between us."

She looked surprised.

"To be honest, Jess, I avoid your type." He went to her. "But, lady, you've been driving me crazy since the moment I first saw you."

She smiled, looking entirely too pleased about the whole situation. "What a nice thing to say."

And frankly he didn't understand any of it. She wasn't his type at all, but he couldn't seem to stay away from Jess Calhoun. "So we've got a problem."

She grew serious. "What do you mean? Are you going to leave? What about Storm?"

He paced away from her, then back again. "No, I'm not leaving. I don't run away from my commitments. But I only commit to the horses I train." He stopped. "You need to know that I don't do well with people relationships."

"You said that before, and I told you I don't expect anything from you."

He let his hands drop to his sides. "You can still get hurt, Jess."

Too late, Jess thought. His words already pierced

her. Her guard went up. "Is that why you came here, to warn me? Fine, consider me warned. Now, you can leave."

"Ah, Jess. That's the problem. I don't want to leave you."

She folded her arms to keep from shaking. It didn't work. "So what do we do now?"

"The hell if I know." He reached for her, all his good intentions to keep away from her falling by the wayside. "All I know right now is I don't want to talk any longer." His mouth came down on hers in a hungry kiss. Immediately, desire surged through his body.

Johnny wanted this woman like no other. That alone was bad, but that didn't stop him as his tongue traced her lips. She parted them, letting him taste what he longed for.

He broke off the kiss, then pressed his forehead against hers. "Ah, Jess, this could lead to trouble."

But all he knew was he didn't want to stop. His mouth covered hers, wanting another taste of her again and again.

"Oh, Johnny," she breathed as her fingers gripped the front of his shirt and reached up to return another kiss.

"Mom!"

Jess tore away from Johnny. "That's Brady." She quickly pulled out of the tight embrace. "I need to go to him," she said, and hurried out of the room.

Johnny sank down on the sofa and closed his eyes, cursing at his weakness. A child's cry reminding him this was a lousy idea.

* * *

Jess walked into her son's room. "What's wrong, honey?"

"I heard a noise. Is someone here?"

"Yes, there is, but you're not to worry about that." She straightened the blankets. "It's time you were asleep."

"But I'm thirsty and I can't stop thinking about my new pony."

She went off to the bathroom to get Brady some water. She took the first drink, and then refilled the glass for her son. Once back she handed Brady the water. He drank about half, then lay back down.

She kissed him and headed for the door. "Mom."

She turned around. "I'm glad Johnny is going to teach me to ride," he said, then rolled over. "Night."

"Night, son."

Jess returned to the living room to see Johnny's head resting against the back of the sofa, his eyes closed. Darn if only she could forget all her responsibilities, and dive into an affair with this man. She had to think about her child first.

She sat down across from him. "He heard us."

Johnny sat up, those gray eyes locked on hers, mesmerizing her again. "What did you tell him?"

"I said someone came by to see me. I didn't mention your name. I'd never get him to stay in bed if he knew you were out here."

"It was probably a bad idea that I came here." He didn't move to get up.

"I need to think about Brady. It would have been awkward if he'd come out here." That was an understatement, but she did have a hard time resisting him, even with her son close by.

"I probably shouldn't come by anymore."

She touched his arm. "I didn't say that. I just don't want Brady to walk in on us. It's hard to explain things to a five-year-old."

His face broke into a grin. "So I better behave myself."

She smiled, too. "Can you do that?"

"If you ask me to, I will." He stood and walked to her, placing a sweet kiss on her lips. "I can't seem to get a decent night's sleep because I keep thinking about you."

Her heart began racing once again and she couldn't come up with anything to say. "I'm sorry."

He pulled her to the entry. "Don't be sorry. You're beautiful dream material, darlin'." He hesitated, then said, "I'm not going to be around long, Jess. When my job ends, I move on."

She wanted so badly to argue with him. She wanted to make him fall for her so he'd never want to leave. Instead, she nodded.

His mouth came down on hers. There was nothing gentle about the kiss. It was hot and demanding, letting her know exactly what he wanted from her.

He broke off. "Sweet dreams, Jess." He turned and walked out the door.

She stood at door, aching for the man who'd just left. She wanted to chase him down and tell him to stay, but in the end, he would leave her. She couldn't hold a man like Johnny Jameson. And how could she risk her heart again knowing it was just a matter of time until he packed up and left her? Too late. She was already halfway in love and she was finding it hard to resist the man.

Two days later in the afternoon, Jess drove to the ranch to pick up Brady. She was surprised to find her son outside in the front yard with Wes. She pulled into the drive at the back door and climbed out.

Brady ran down the steps. "Mom, you're home. We've been waiting and waiting."

She caught her son in a hug. "Waiting for what?"

"They're here. The ponies are here. But Wes said I can't go near them until you got here."

The foreman came up to her. "Hi, Jess. I guess Brady told you the news."

This was happening too fast. "Fill in the blanks for me, please."

Wes nodded. "Sure. I went over to the Carson Ranch today. Harry showed me the ponies and convinced me to take them both home and let Brady decide which one he wants. I swear the man wouldn't let me get a word in and before I knew what was happening he'd hitched up the trailer and loaded in the two ponies."

Brady jumped in. "Sassy and Beau are here and I get to choose one." Her son's eyes were round. "Mom, can I see them now?"

She loved seeing her son's excitement. She looked back at Wes.

"I tried to get ahold of you, but I got your voice mail. I called the bakery and you'd left. I wouldn't have brought them home if we hadn't talked about it."

"I know." She smiled at her son. "Okay, then let's go see them."

They all headed toward the horse barn. "They're New Forest ponies," Wes told her. "Harry got them for his grandkids, but they moved away and he doesn't want them neglected. I put them in the large stall. They seemed to like being together."

Jess held her son's hand. She couldn't tell if he was nervous or just excited. They were just inside the doors when she spotted Johnny coming toward them. He moved in a slow, easy gait, a loose-hipped swagger that most cowboys tried to pull off, but Johnny had it perfected. He oozed sex appeal. He affected her in ways she never knew possible. Her body seemed to come alive whenever the man was around.

"Johnny," her son cried as he motioned for him to join them.

Jess tensed as he made his way toward them. She hadn't seen him since he left her apartment two nights ago. Memories flooded back, along with so many confusing feelings for this man.

"Hey, partner," he greeted Brady, then he looked at her. "Hi, Jess."

"Hello, Johnny."

He turned his attention to Brady. "Hey, did you know there are two ponies in the barn?"

The boy nodded. "They're for me! I get to pick one for my birthday."

Johnny knelt in front of Brady. "Don't be too quick to choose. Your first horse is important. He or she is going to be a good friend, and you need to see that you get along."

"Oh. You mean I might not like them."

"No, I mean, you should feel comfortable with your mount."

"Then will you help me?" the boy asked. "I might be a little scared."

Johnny smiled. "Of course, but once you get to know the pony, you'll feel a lot better. Wes wouldn't bring you an animal that wasn't gentle."

Brady looked up at the foreman and smiled. "Can I see them now, Wes?"

The foreman nodded. Jess was not only surprised with Brady's eagerness, but also when he took Johnny's hand like it was the most natural thing in the world.

The painful part was it wasn't the same for Johnny. This was a temporary stop for the horse trainer. She followed the group to the double stall. Johnny lifted Brady to the railing to get a good look at the ponies.

"Oh, Mom, look!"

Jess admired the shiny coat of the reddish-brown gelding. She wasn't an expert about this breed. They were definitely bigger than a Shetland pony.

"The chestnut is Beau," Wes informed them. "The buckskin is Sassy."

She looked at her son, unable to know what to do. This was one of those times she wanted her dad's advice.

Johnny opened the gate and went inside, trying to focus on the ponies and not Jess. She'd distracted him, more than ever since the last time they were together.

Right away the chestnut gelding came to him. He spoke quietly to the horse, then reached out and stroked him. He was average height for this breed, about thirteen hands high.

Johnny liked Beau right off. He was the friendlier of the two. Sassy was a little skittish. But it was up to the kid.

"Which one do you like, Brady?"

"Beau."

Johnny took a rope off the hook, snapped it on the pony's bridle and led him out of the stall. "Okay, let's try him out."

Brady looked a little frightened. "Right now?"

"Don't see any better time. At least, let's get him outside so I can see how he acts around people. Maybe we'll save the riding for another day."

The boy nodded and followed behind with his mother and Wes. Once in the corral, Johnny put the animal through some simple commands and was happy to see how well trained he was.

"Did Carson say if the animal has any bad habits?"

Wes shook his head, watching closely. "Harry said that Beau is a peach. Sassy is good, too, but she can be a little high-strung."

Johnny saw how Brady clung to his mother. This wasn't going to be easy. "How about we pet him first?"

He eyed Jess as she coaxed her son closer. "First thing we do is let your horse know you're around so not to spook him, but talk quietly. Animals don't like to have someone sneak up on them. So start talking to him."

"Hi, Beau." Brady edged closer. "I want to be your friend." He held out his hand and when he was close enough the pony turned his way. "I'm Brady."

The animal bobbed his head and took a step closer. The boy backed off. That was when Johnny swung Brady up into his arms. "Okay, let's get you up to be his size."

Johnny felt a strange feeling go through him as he held the child close, and reassured him that he wouldn't let anything happen to him.

Brady reached out and petted the pony's forehead. "He's soft."

"Yes, he is." With Wes holding the reins, Johnny carried Brady around the animal, letting him get to know the dos and don'ts of being around a horse. Johnny rubbed the horse's coat across his back and neck. Brady followed suit and the horse enjoyed the attention. Beau bobbed his head again and blew air out of his nostrils.

"See, he likes it."

Brady giggled. Then Johnny convinced the boy to take the reins and walk the animal around the corral. Of course, Johnny was right with him. He smiled when the horse followed like a trained dog.

They returned to the barn door. "That was fun," Brady announced. "Mom, can I ride Beau tomorrow?"

Her son's sudden change surprised her. "Why don't we wait and see?"

"Maybe first I should try him out," Johnny offered.

"Good idea," she told him. "Brady, you go up to the house and tell Nancy I'll be there in a minute."

"Okay," her son said, then turned to Johnny and Wes. "Thanks, Wes, for bringing the ponies. And thanks, Johnny, for helping me with Beau."

"Any time," Johnny said.

Wes said, "You're welcome, Brady. Hold on and I'll walk you to the house."

"I'll take Beau back to the stall," Johnny said.

As Jess watched the two walk off, she told herself that she wanted to talk with Johnny about the pony. But she knew the truth was she just wanted to talk to him. Period. It had been a long two days. And he hadn't made any effort to get ahold of her. She hated to admit it, but she'd been disappointed, especially after the kisses they'd shared in her apartment.

Once the horse was back in the stall, Johnny stroked both the animals, before he finally exited through the gate. Jess was waiting for him.

"Is Beau really a good mount for Brady?"

"I don't see a problem with the pony. It's Brady who needs more confidence. The more time he spends around the horse, the better."

"I'm happy he wants to try. Thank you."

"I haven't done anything yet." He moved in closer and smiled. "But if it enables me to spend more time with you, I'm glad."

He leaned down and placed a gentle kiss across her mouth. It was slow and easy, but it got her heart pounding.

He pulled back. "Sorry, I tried but I couldn't resist."

"Oh…" Her voice sounded squeaky and she wanted nothing more than to be in Johnny's arms.

Three ranch hands walked in at the far end of the barn and she stepped back. Johnny took her by the arm and walked her down the aisle past Storm's stall to where he kept his horse.

"Since it's still early I'm going to take Risky for some exercise. You want to ride along?"

She couldn't help herself when it came to this man. "Sure. I'll see if Nancy can watch Brady."

Fifteen minutes later, Johnny stood at the corral railing holding the reins to his bay roan, Risky, and the buckskin, Goldie, and second-guessing his invitation to Jess. He needed to stay away, not get closer.

Then he saw her come out of the house, and all common sense flew out the window. She'd changed into a pair of jeans and boots and placed a hat on her head. By the time she reached him the cold air had colored her cheeks…and her mouth.

"You saddled Goldie."

"It saves time."

"Thank you." She took the reins, and climbed on the mare.

They headed out of the corral and Johnny glanced across at Jess. She was a natural on horseback with a good seat and straight back.

"Is Goldie your horse?"

She nodded. "I got her in high school. I used to barrel race back then. I feel bad because I don't have the time or energy to ride her like I should."

They picked up the pace to a canter. "That's a shame because it looks like you really enjoy it."

Jess couldn't help but smile as they rode. The easy rocking motion was relaxing, the scenery gorgeous.

"I do, but my son and the business keep me pretty busy."

"Maybe soon Brady will be able to ride with you."

Johnny was curious. "Do you know what caused Brady's fear to begin with?"

"I think Dad just got overly anxious and he pushed Brady at too young an age." She glanced at him. "He did pretty well today, though. The first time he'd touched a horse was the day you arrived."

Risky danced sideways, eager to run. "You want to pick up the pace?"

"Sure."

"You lead the way," he told her.

Jess pushed her hat down and kicked her heels against the mare's sides, then shot off. That was all Risky needed and he was soon after them. Johnny watched as Jess's head lowered and she moved in perfect unison with the racing horse. He came up beside her and enjoyed the view of the woman in motion. They didn't stop until they saw the creek.

Reaching the bank, Jess climbed down, smiling as she walked her mount to the water. "Wow, I haven't ridden like that in years."

"You're good."

"I'm Clay Calhoun's daughter. I'm supposed to be a good rider."

"I know you miss him."

She walked with him through the stiff winter grass to the tree. "It's hard to imagine the Double Bar C going on without him. He loved this land." She glanced around the landscape. "Now, Holt runs the operation, as you know, but he'll be gone awhile." She released a breath. "I have to say we miss his leadership. There are so many things I could use his help on."

He frowned. "Is there anything I can do?"

"Thank you. You're handling Storm—that's a big enough help. It's just that it would be nice to have my brothers and sister here. I miss them." She looked at him. "Do you have any siblings?"

He shook his head. "None that I know of."

"What about your father? Did you have any luck tracking him down?" she asked.

He shook his head. "No. I tried for years, but I never could catch up with him."

He caught the sadness etched on her face. "Johnny, I'm sorry."

He hated pity. He especially didn't want it from her. "Why? You had nothing to do with it. Jake Jameson just didn't want to be found, or meet his son." He shrugged. "Hey, you can't miss what you've never had. I'm not much of a homebody, either. I guess that's why I like to keep moving, to have the freedom of changing my mind whenever I want."

"So you won't be here to meet Holt when he gets back?"

Johnny looked into her eyes and felt a twinge of regret. No regrets, he had to leave. It would be better for everyone. "Depends when that is but I kind of doubt it."

He watched as Jess pushed the braid off her shoulder. He enjoyed watching the simple action from this beautiful woman.

"Seems strange that you've perfected your skill and yet you still like moving around."

Johnny blew out a breath. "I'm used to it. As a kid, my mother changed locations all the time, until she met a guy." His boot heel dug at the dry grass. "That was when I took off."

She looked at him. "You couldn't have been that old."

"Old enough to know when to get away from a bad situation. I've been going it alone for a long time now."

Jess looked out over the land. "I guess that's where we're different. I've never really lived anywhere else. Outside of a few years at college, I haven't been a lot of places."

"Why should you want to leave? You have your business here and your home."

She smiled. "I had to fight Dad to live on my own. But I've got a little Calhoun stubbornness, too."

"And you got all the beauty."

She shook her head. "You should see my younger sister, Megan. She's the real beauty in the family."

"Man, I can't imagine she's any lovelier than you." Johnny came closer, removing her hat, and studied her face. "Your eyes are incredible, sometimes brown, other times green. And your mouth... I could kiss you for hours."

She sucked in a breath and raised her gaze to his. "Johnny, I thought... We weren't going to do this."

He rested his forearm above her head on the tree trunk. "You don't want me to kiss you anymore?"

"It's just... I'm not sure we should start this."

"Don't look now, darlin', but it's already started."

"I know, but...maybe we should set some ground rules."

She looked at him with those big eyes and he found he wanted to change her mind.

"You mean like keeping us a secret?"

She shook her head. "No, I'm single and you're single so we're doing nothing wrong if we're seeing each other."

"Darlin', I want to do a lot more than just see you."

She couldn't stop the blush. She wanted the same thing but she had to think about her son. "It's just Brady. If he sees us together, he might get ideas. So maybe we shouldn't broadcast us being together."

He paused, then said, "I wish I could give you more, Jess. So I wouldn't blame you if you want me to keep my distance."

Jess only knew she should tell him yes, but the problem was, she wanted this man. "No. That won't be necessary. No strings, no expectations, is probably better, then no one gets hurt," she said, not even believing her own words. This was so out of her comfort zone. She felt the familiar fear creeping back. But Johnny Jameson had her wanting things.

He nodded. "So you want to take a chance with this cowboy?"

Oh, boy, she was in trouble now. But she couldn't seem to turn him down. "Maybe I would."

CHAPTER SEVEN

AN HOUR later they rode back to the barn. Johnny walked Risky to his stall, removed his tack and filled his feed bag. Jess had to hand her horse over to one of the men when she'd gotten a call from the bakery. Then she hurried off to the house and her son.

After he finished with his horse, Johnny went up to his apartment and saw that Jess's car was gone. This was all backfiring in his face. He wanted a fling and she was willing to go along. They were going to spend time together. He should be happy with the no-strings relationship. Except for one thing. He was afraid that Jess Calhoun was becoming too special.

After opening the door to his apartment, he walked in and headed to the refrigerator. There wasn't much inside, just some milk and lunch meat for a sandwich.

He closed the door, and dropped onto the sofa. He'd been spoiled by Nancy and Jess's cooking so not much else sounded good. But with those meals came strings—Jess and her son.

Getting up, he went to the dresser and opened the top drawer. After digging through his stack of underwear, he came up with a black velvet box. He opened the lid to find a single, square-cut diamond.

He thought back to three years ago and the nice girl he left in Dallas. Amy was the daughter of one of the ranchers he'd worked for. They'd dated for a while, and suddenly he found himself buying a ring and getting down on one knee.

Not long after, he felt that his life was being planned out for him. It was decided where they'd live, what house, where he'd work. He realized suddenly he didn't want any of it. Or he did want it, but dammit, he was afraid to get too close. A familiar painful ache in his chest had stopped him just in time. The one thing he'd always longed for had been the one thing he feared. He'd reached out too many times as a kid and had been turned away. The scars served as a reminder that he wasn't cut out for love. He was so afraid to lose it again.

He couldn't go through with the marriage. Worse, he had to tell Amy. She threw the ring back in his face and he left town.

He wasn't proud of what he'd done, but it was better than him walking away after they'd married. He snapped closed the box's lid. It was a symbol, a reminder, to keep things light.

No more promises that he couldn't keep. Because in the end, he always left. He'd been in situations like this a few times before, and knew how to avoid them.

Of course that was before he ran headlong into Jess Calhoun.

The next morning, Jess walked Brady inside his classroom at the preschool. Before she left, the teacher, Liz Peterson, pulled her aside.

"I wanted to give you a flyer." She handed her the

single sheet of paper that read "Little Buckaroos First Annual Rodeo, Saturday, January 28".

Jess was surprised. How long had this been going on? "I thought you were having a bake sale."

"It's been in the works awhile. We called a parent meeting at the first part of December. Then we discovered the cost of new computers and playground equipment," the teacher told her. The pretty brunette had a lot of enthusiasm and it showed with the kids.

That wasn't long after Clay's death. "I'm sorry I didn't make it. There's been a lot going on." She waved a hand at her excuse. "What kind of rodeo are we talking about?" Jess asked.

Liz could hardly contain herself. "It's for both adults and children but on a small scale, of course. The events for the adults are Tie Down Roping, Team Roping and Barrel Racing. For the children, it's Mutton Bustin'."

Jess knew about the kids' rodeo. They had to be under sixty pounds and would be riding sheep.

"It's strictly for amateurs, only small cash prizes. We're hoping to get a lot of families involved." Liz's eyes grew wider as she spoke. "It's going to be at the Larkville Corral. We're hoping you'll still want to donate some baked goods to sale."

"Of course." At least she could do that much. "And let me know if there is anything else you need."

"Maybe see if you can convince some of your ranch hands to sign up."

She nodded. "I'll see what I can do. Give me more flyers and I'll hand them out."

Liz gave her another dozen. "Cheyenne and Derrick

Carson are chairing the committee, so they can give you all the details."

Jess read the flyer and could see that the committee had been busy. "It looks pretty organized."

"Yes, but we need all the merchants to help out. This money is also shared with the church charities. We're hoping this will set an example to the kids and we want them to help as much as possible."

That would be a good lesson. "You can count on me. Molly and I can set up a sweet booth and we'll donate all the profits."

"Oh, Jess, that would be wonderful."

"Have Cheyenne get in touch with me, and we'll go from there."

Jess walked away smiling. This was the first time she was involved in a school fundraiser for her child. She thought about her family. They weren't here to help her, but Wes and Nancy would, of course. She thought about Johnny, wondering if he would still be here for it, too.

She'd be lying if she said that it didn't matter. It did. She wanted Johnny Jameson to stay. She'd never met a man who made her feel this way. She thought back to her first serious boyfriend, Brady's father, Chad Branson. They'd both been such kids. Okay, she'd thought she loved Chad. Yet in the end, she'd been glad that she didn't marry a man who would eventually break her young heart, and Brady's, too.

She climbed in her car and started the engine. Her thoughts returned to the man who'd kept her awake nights. Who had her longing for things she never wanted before. Maybe she'd just been too shy to ask for them. Even knowing he would be leaving, she still couldn't stay away from Johnny.

At least this time, she knew the rules and she could protect her heart.

Johnny had just finished his session with Storm, and put him in his stall, when he came out of the barn to see Brady running toward him.

"Johnny! Johnny!"

Johnny caught the charging kid in his arms and lifted him up. "Whoa, partner. Where are you headed with that full head of steam?"

"To talk to you. Look." He shoved a piece of paper at him. "It's our school rodeo. Now I hafta learn to ride 'cause I need to be in it. If I can learn to ride real good, then I can ride Beau in the opening part and carry a flag. Please help me."

Johnny set the boy down and looked over the paper. "Well, this doesn't give us much time." He continued to read. "What's this Mutton Bustin'?"

"That's if you're little like me, you get to ride a sheep instead of a bull."

"Now you want to ride a sheep?"

The boy nodded. "If you show me how? And I need someone to be in it with me. Will you do that, too?"

Johnny felt something tugging in his chest. He knew the kid looked up to him. "Whoa, son, I might be able to come up with a sheep to practice with, but I'm not a rodeo cowboy."

"Well, you can do something with Risky. Does he do some tricks? And you can help me ride Beau, too."

He liked the kid's enthusiasm. "That's a lot of work. You haven't even been on Beau yet."

"I really want to do it."

He looked up and saw Jess approach them. "I see he's told you about the rodeo," she said.

Johnny nodded. "It's a tall order in a short time span."

"You can do it, Johnny," Brady said, smiling, then turned to his mother. "Mom, are you going to barrel race? Papa said you were the best. Oh, I've got to go tell Wes." He took off toward the foreman coming out of the barn.

"That's a lot of words to come out of such a little guy."

"I think this fundraiser has a lot to do with his excitement," she said. "And for whatever reason, you and his new pony are his new focus."

Johnny didn't want anyone looking up to him. It would only cause disappointment. "Look, Jess. Brady's a great kid, but I could be gone by then."

"I know, but maybe you won't be." She walked closer. "Doesn't give you much time left to enjoy your stay here." Her gaze met his and he felt a stirring. "You should at least get to know the people of Larkville."

He covered her hand with his. "I'd rather get to know you."

"It might be arranged," she told him.

He smiled at her playfulness. "I thought maybe we can spend some time together."

"What do you have in mind?"

He had trouble swallowing. Damn, if she wasn't the most tempting woman. He glanced around to see several men doing chores. Although not in earshot, no doubt they could see him and Jess. So he kept his hands to himself.

"That's up to you," he said, throwing the challenge back to her.

She smiled. "Why don't you come by tonight and we'll see how the evening turns out?"

This was becoming a habit. Another supper and Johnny might as well move into the main ranch house. He did spend some time with Brady and his new pony. He'd gotten the kid to sit on Beau bareback, and it seemed to go fine. He'd promised the boy tomorrow that he'd put a saddle on the pony and they could walk around the corral.

Most of the dinner conversation centered around the boy, but Johnny kept getting distracted as Jess sat across from him. Tonight it was only the three of them because Nancy had gone off with Wes to a movie. Maybe it was a little too cozy.

Jess started clearing plates while Brady went into the connecting family room to watch a video. Johnny followed Jess into the kitchen to help.

He stood next to her at the sink. "If you keep feeding me like this, I won't be able to get my jeans fastened."

Jess's gaze went to his flat stomach. "You look like you're doing fine to me."

"I guess I'll work it off. There's a nice gym at the bunkhouse." He leaned closer, placing the empty plates in the soapy water. "Is that because you supply all the crew with desserts?"

She glanced at him, so close he could lean down and

kiss her. Then she turned away. "No, it's because the strength training helps with the hard physical labor." She began rinsing dishes. "And no one is forced to work out."

Over the past two weeks he had learned firsthand that the Double Bar C was a top-notch operation. The men who worked here were paid well, but were also expected to do a good job. There were no slackers. Living quarters were nice, with a lot of room and good food. Yeah, it would be hard to leave here.

"Brady had a good day. He let me put him atop Beau and we walked around the corral."

She smiled and his breath caught. "He told me. Several times. I can't thank you enough. My dad would have loved this. He always felt guilty that he might have been the one to cause Brady's fears."

Johnny shrugged. "Who's to say. Your son is older now. We'll see what happens. I know it's been hard for you to stay away, but I think Brady wants to get a little better before he invites you down."

He kept talking, hoping it would distract him from what he really wanted to do, but it didn't help. He finally leaned in and his mouth covered hers. He kissed her slow and tender, holding back as best he could. He pulled back and saw the heat in her eyes, then went back for more. This time, he wrapped his arms around her waist and drew her close.

She must have liked it, because her hands moved over his chest and his neck and she opened up to him. She tasted of coffee and pure, sweet Jess.

"Mom? Why are you kissing Johnny?"

Jess gasped and pulled away. "Brady! I didn't hear you come in."

The little boy glanced back and forth between the two. "My friend Cody says his dad and mom kiss a lot."

Jess answered quickly. "Johnny and I are friends. I like him and he likes me. And sometimes adults kiss. Hey, you should get your things together and we need to head home."

The child nodded, but not before he eyed Johnny carefully. Johnny didn't blame the kid. The boy was watching out for his mother.

Soon the dishes were done, and Johnny helped Brady put away his toys and get his coat on. They headed for the back door.

"Johnny," the boy said. "It's okay if you kiss Mom. Now that Papa is gone to heaven, she needs more kisses."

Johnny winked at Jess, who seemed embarrassed by her son's perception. "Thank you, Brady. I can see that she does." He leaned forward and placed a tender kiss on Jess's mouth. "Thanks for supper."

"You're welcome. Good night."

He leaned down to Brady and swept him up into his arms in a big hug. "How was that, kiddo?"

"Good," the boy admitted, and Johnny realized that Brady's approval meant far too much to him.

Two evenings later, Johnny asked Jess out to dinner. With limited options on restaurants, he took her into town to the Saddle Up Bar and Grill. The place was crowded, standing-room-only in the bar.

The restaurant had a rustic quality, open beam ceiling and scarred hardwood floors. There was a big stone fireplace in the entry area where they stood waiting for their table.

Jess wore her thick blond curls down against her shoulders. It was a big contrast with the dark rust-colored sweater that hugged her curves. A denim skirt hung to just below her knees, and buckskin boots finished the outfit.

He swallowed hard, wanting nothing more than to get her out of here.

Instead, he stood by her side as she greeted and introduced him to several friends. Everyone was curious about him, just like they'd been at the dance at the Cattleman's Club.

Why not? Clay Calhoun had been a beloved man in this town. A good neighbor and a good friend to everyone. If something was needed, Clay stepped up to help. So if someone was interested in his daughter, the townspeople wanted to make sure he was acceptable.

And Johnny Jameson wasn't anywhere close to being worthy of Jess Calhoun. Yet, that didn't stop him from wanting to spend time with her.

"Your table's ready, sir," the hostess said.

"Thank you." Johnny pressed his hand against Jess's back and escorted her through the crowd. In the dining room, they passed by another large fireplace, stopping to greet more people, then finally they reached their table by the window.

Jess slid into the black vinyl booth. "Sorry. It's a small town."

"You don't have to apologize."

The candle on the table illumined her bright smile

and incredible honey-brown eyes. She leaned forward
and said, "To be honest, I don't go out much. Not on
dates, anyway." She hesitated. "Not since Brady's
father…Chad. So I think the citizens in Larkville are
a little shocked to see you out with me."

He thought, not for the first time, that he couldn't
believe the men in this town wouldn't be after her in a
flash. "I'm a lucky guy, then. I'm glad you chose me
to spend time with."

The waitress arrived at the table. "Would you like
to order?" she asked them.

Johnny looked at Jess. "I think we should celebrate
your coming out tonight." He ordered a bottle of wine
to go along with their steaks.

Jess wasn't sure what she was doing here with someone like Johnny. She was too inexperienced for the
man. With Chad they'd been kids. She couldn't even
drink legally. Now, it felt as if everyone in the place
was watching them. And no doubt there would be more
talk when Johnny left town.

She leaned across the table and said softly, "This
must be uncomfortable for you."

"Why?"

"I bet you're not used to being watched while you
eat your dinner."

Johnny was a handsome man, and even more so
when he smiled. "They're just jealous because I'm with
the prettiest woman in the room."

She smiled. "You are a charmer, Johnny Jameson.
You don't need—"

He stopped her words. "It's a shame some man
hasn't shown you how special you are long before now.

I plan to correct that…soon." He surprised her when he reached for her hand and held it in his. She could feel the warmth, and the slight roughness. She sucked in a breath, remembering how those hands felt against her skin.

He leaned closer. "You have no idea how much I wish we were alone."

"You shouldn't say that so fast. You have no idea how good their steaks are," she said, trying to make light of his words.

He started to speak when a young couple stopped by the table. "Jess! How wonderful to see you," the pretty brunette said, then turned to Johnny.

Jess pulled her hand away. She didn't need this now. "Oh, Cheyenne. It's nice to see you, too."

The woman eyed Johnny closely. "It seems strange to see you out…"

Jess hurried on to say, "Johnny Jameson, this is Cheyenne and Derrick Carson. Brady goes to school with their son, Tucker. They're also chairing the rodeo."

Johnny immediately stood and shook their hands. "The rodeo is all that Brady talks about."

Cheyenne's arched an eyebrow. "Oh, is he going to participate?" The woman glanced at Jess before turning back to Johnny. "Poor thing has always been so deathly afraid of horses. It had to be such a trial for Clayton."

"From what I understand," Johnny began, "nothing that boy could do would ever be anything but perfect in his grandfather's eyes."

Cheyenne looked surprised. "So you've met Clayton."

Johnny glanced at Jess and winked. "Yes, I've had

the honor of meeting the man. In fact, he's the one who hired me."

Derrick finally stepped in. "You're the horse trainer."

"I am. I've been working with Night Storm."

"How is that going?" Derrick asked.

"It's coming along."

Cheyenne spoke up again. "I hope you enjoy your stay here, Johnny. Maybe even enter in our rodeo. It's all for charity."

The waitress arrived with their salads.

"I'll think about it," Johnny said. "Right now our dinner has arrived, so if you'll excuse us."

"Of course. It was nice to meet you." Cheyenne turned to Jess. "I'll give you a call later." The couple walked off, and Jess let out a long breath.

After the salads were placed on the table and the wine was served, they were finally alone.

"Is Cheyenne Carson a friend of yours?"

Jess shook her head. "Not really. We went to school together. You know the type. The most popular—head cheerleader, homecoming queen and dated the captain of the football team. That would be Derrick."

"Too bad you didn't give her a run for her money. You would have beaten her at all of it." He took a drink of his wine. "You have to know she envies you."

She needed a drink and took it. "Why?"

"Because you're beautiful, successful and have a wonderful son."

"She has Derrick and two kids."

He arched an eyebrow. "You want Derrick?"

"No!" She wanted Johnny Jameson. "He's self-centered and thinks he's God's gift to women."

Johnny was grinning now. "Seems to me those two are made for each other."

She couldn't look him in the eye. Did he know she wanted them to be made for each other, too?

CHAPTER EIGHT

I⊤ ᴡᴀs just after ten o'clock when Johnny drove Jess back to her apartment. Yet, seeing how nervous she was acting, he wasn't going to push her into anything.

He pulled up next to her car. "How about some dessert?"

She stared at him. "You didn't want dessert at the restaurant."

"I wanted your dessert. What's the fun of owning a bakery and not being able to raid the place?"

She finally smiled. "I'm closed tomorrow, but there might be some leftovers in the fridge."

"Now you're talking."

They got out of his truck and walked around to the back door of the shop. Jess unlocked the door and flipped on the under-counter lights. Walking to the large refrigerator, she removed her coat, then opened the door to find two pies and a carrot cake.

"Oh, pie!" Johnny said as he removed his jacket and hat. "What kind?"

"There's apple and chocolate."

"Chocolate."

Jess took out the pie, put it on the counter and then got plates and forks. She cut them each a piece and placed a dollop of whipped cream on each, then handed him his plate.

"Thank you."

He dug in and she found she liked watching him. Even the simple things, like the way he chewed, his Adam's apple bobbing as he swallowed. He looked at her and she froze.

"You aren't eating." He cut a piece of his and offered it to her.

Jess opened her mouth to accept the offering. She couldn't have said what it tasted like because she was too mesmerized by Johnny's actions.

"It's good, huh?"

She nodded.

"I think I need another taste." He set down the plate, and lowered his head. "This way," he breathed as his mouth closed over hers. He then pulled back and looked her in the eyes. "It was good before, but so much better when your flavor is mixed in."

Jess finally drew air into her lungs, feeling more daring now. She managed to scoop up a piece of her pie and offered it to him. He took it.

"Let's see if you're right," she said, then leaned toward him and placed her mouth against his.

With a groan, he pulled her against him and deepened the kiss. She went willingly into his arms as her mouth opened and he dove inside, moving his tongue over hers, and her need for him grew stronger.

"Damn, you even taste better than the pie." He lifted her up on the counter, and went back again for another taste.

Jess was drowning in the man. She felt his hands

move over her back, then he slipped them under her sweater.

He broke off the kiss, but his hands were still working their magic. "I've wanted to touch you like this all night," he confessed.

She locked her arms around his neck, unable to slow her own breathing. "I wanted you to touch me, too."

"Looks like we're getting our wish." He kissed her again, then pulled up her sweater, exposing her lacy bra. When he touched her again, she moaned softly.

He raised his head. "Jess, I'm not going to survive much more. I want you too much." His mouth covered hers again. Then suddenly the mood was shattered when her cell phone rang. She broke off the kiss, pulled down her sweater as she dug through her purse. "It could be about Brady."

Johnny nodded and stepped away. He needed to get himself under control.

"Hello," Jess spoke into the phone. "Oh, Holt. No, I wasn't home. Sorry, I didn't know that I had to be in by nine." She looked over at him and mouthed, *My brother.* "Yes, I had dinner with a friend."

Johnny turned away as she slid off the counter. He was a friend. Of course, what else would she tell her brother? That she was in her lover's arms? *Was he going to be her lover?* He knew this would be a big step for Jess. He also saw how protective everyone in town was toward her.

And here he was, at the first opportunity, taking advantage of her. Great. He glanced at her as she turned away and pulled down her sweater farther. He was trying to get her naked in the kitchen. Jess Calhoun deserved better.

Then why couldn't he walk away from her? Jess looked at him and smiled and his heart began to drum in his chest once more.

She finally hung up. "Sorry, that was Holt. When he couldn't get ahold of me, he got worried. Big brothers." She shook her head. "I hate him sometimes, but I love him for always being there for me."

"If you were my sister, I'd be worried, too. My intentions aren't exactly honorable."

In the span of a phone call things seemed to have cooled off between them. Good or bad, it gave Jess some time to try and think. She didn't seem to be able to think sensibly when it came to Johnny Jameson. And she needed to do just that. Think. It had been a long time since she let herself care about a man. Yet, without a second thought, she'd been willing to give herself to him.

They climbed the steps to her apartment and she unlocked the door. Once inside, she hung her coat on the hook. She turned around to find that Johnny hadn't moved from the entry.

"I think I should head back to the ranch," he told her. "We both have an early start tomorrow. I had a great time tonight, Jess. Thank you."

That hurt her feelings. "I had a great time, too." When he started to turn toward the door, she called to him, "Don't go, Johnny."

He looked at her with those silver-gray eyes. "If I don't, Jess, we'll finish what we started downstairs. I don't think you're ready for that."

She shivered at the thought. He wanted her. "Maybe…"

He came to her. "It can't be a maybe, brown eyes. The last thing I want is for you to have regrets."

She wouldn't, but maybe he would. "Then could you stay for coffee? I want to talk to you about something."

He frowned. "What?"

She had to think fast. "Brady's eagerness to ride a horse for one, and Holt mentioned to me on the phone to see if you're interested in looking at two other horses."

Johnny was about to decline the offer when Jess turned and headed for the small kitchen. Okay, he could handle some coffee, but he needed to keep this light. It was getting too intense.

He walked to a desk and saw the row of pictures. He smiled, seeing different stages of Brady's growth. Jess came up beside him.

"He's a cute kid," he told her.

She smiled. "I think so." She picked up one photo with Clay and Sandra Calhoun. "This is a favorite of mine. That's my mother."

Johnny studied the attractive brunette. "She's pretty. You look like her."

"I've been told that. She's the one who really got me interested in baking." She looked at Johnny. "We were all pretty devastated, especially Dad, when she died so suddenly." She shrugged. "Sometimes I wonder if that's the reason he didn't take care of himself. I know he missed her terribly." She put the picture back on the counter. "Now we've lost both of them. Brady's lost the most, his best friend." He saw the tears gather in her eyes.

"Hey, darlin', I didn't mean to make you cry." He hated to see her so sad.

"It's just that Clay Calhoun was the total family man. There was no doubt he loved us kids. I always knew I was so lucky to have him as my dad."

Johnny was glad someone had family. Maybe that was why he related to the boy so well.

"I'm sorry, Jess. For both you and Brady."

"Don't be. I could never regret having my son, but Chad was nowhere close to taking on fatherhood. Thank God I had my mom and dad to help me."

"And you should treasure your family," he told her.

She sighed. "Speaking of that, I wish they'd come home soon."

Dealing with Holt Calhoun would take away the temptation of seeing Jess every day. "Did your brother say when he would return?"

She shook her head. "He doesn't know. He's with his friend, Hank Garnett, who's really bad off. It's sad because he's so young but so sick."

He was getting too involved with her life. "That's too bad…. So you wanted to talk to me about something," he reminded her.

She nodded. "Brady. I know he sounded enthusiastic about it but just because this rodeo came up, that doesn't mean you have to help him with that, too."

The timer went off on the coffeemaker, and she went into the kitchen and poured two cups. She handed one to him as he walked up to the bar and sat down on one of the stools.

"I don't have a problem with giving the boy a few extra hours, Jess, unless you have a problem with it?"

She shrugged. "Only the fact that he's barely five, and he's growing more attached to you. I can't help worry he might get hurt when you leave."

Johnny was surprised, but he understood. "So you want me to stay away? To make an excuse as to why I can't do it?"

"Oh, no!" She shook her head. "Besides Wes, you're the only other male figure in his life right now." She blinked hard. "I'm just saying he misses his grandfather." She sighed. "I guess I want to protect him from all hurt, but I know I can't."

Johnny stood, rounded the counter and drew her into his arms. She was breaking his heart. "Shh, darlin', it's going be okay. Brady and I will work things out when the time comes for me to leave."

She nodded and wiped her eyes. "Sorry I got all emotional. I'm fiercely protective of my son."

He would love to hold her anytime. He was trying not to think about thirty minutes ago when he'd been kissing her. "Not a problem. I better go. I've got a date with a stubborn horse in the morning." He headed to the door. "I'll work with Brady tomorrow if you bring him by."

"Thank you, and please come to the house for supper."

Even though he knew he needed to keep it light, so much time with Jess was giving him ideas. Ideas, like maybe Larkville, Texas, would make a pretty nice place to hang around. He quickly brushed aside the thought.

The next afternoon's weather turned sunny, bringing the winter temperature up to a comfortable sixty degrees. Johnny had Brady sitting in a saddle on Beau. That was the easy part. The gelding turned out to be a great mount and the boy was doing well.

In the confines of the corral, Johnny gave the child the reins, and told him to take the horse to the end and back again. This time he wasn't going to walk beside him.

"By myself?"

Johnny nodded. "Sure. You can do it."

Brady took the reins and laid them across the pony's neck, causing him to turn. The boy made the clicking sound with his tongue and the horse walked off.

Johnny watched closely to see if there were any problems. There didn't seem to be any. The child looked good in the saddle. He was a fast learner, and eager for more. Brady returned and Johnny was going to the next step.

"Okay, you did great."

The boy grinned. "I want to go faster."

"That'll take a little longer. And it's going to feel funny at first, but soon you'll learn to bounce with the horse."

"Oh, boy. Teach me how to bounce."

Johnny had to smile at the kid's determination. He took the reins and told Brady to hold on to the pommel just to get the feel of it. Once Johnny took off running he instructed Brady how to go with the horse. Not too bad for the first try. By the time they got back, they were both grinning.

Johnny suddenly had a better idea. He had the ranch hand Randy saddle Risky. Once his horse was brought out, he asked, "Want to go for a ride on my horse with me?"

He saw the hesitation on the boy's face. Johnny left Risky tied at the railing and went to Brady. "Okay, son. There's nothing wrong with being a little afraid, but if you're cautious around a horse, you won't get hurt. And you're still a little guy, so they're going to look a lot bigger. As you grow, they'll look smaller."

Those trusting eyes looked up at him. "And I won't be so afraid."

He nodded. "So for a few more years just stick to the pony."

"I like Beau a lot."

"Would you do something for me? Let me take you riding just so I can show you how to move with the horse."

"You'll hold me real tight?"

"Yep. I wouldn't let anything happen to you."

Once the boy agreed, Johnny took him off Beau and lifted him up onto Risky's saddle, then quickly climbed on behind him. Randy swung open the wide gate of the corral and Johnny walked Risky out to the trail leading to the open pasture.

"Here, you take the reins." Johnny could control the horse with just leg pressure if need be, but he wanted the boy to feel in control.

He explained to Brady his plans, made sure the boy was secure in the saddle, then gave the command to Risky and the horse took off in a trot. Johnny helped Brady find the rhythm, and soon, he was doing better.

"Make Risky go really fast," Brady called out.

Johnny was surprised. "You sure?"

"Yeah, I want to go fast."

"All right, here we go." He made a clicking sound with his mouth and kicked his heels. The horse shot off. With his arms securing the child in the saddle, he had the boy lean downward as the horse ran across the pasture. He was rewarded with a giggle.

Finally Johnny circled Risky around and was coming back when he discovered another rider. He slowed when he recognized Jess on Goldie. She was covering some serious ground until she finally caught up to them.

"Mom! Did you see me riding?"

"Sure did."

She looked at Johnny. "I saddled up to ride with Brady, but by the time I got to the corral, you were gone."

"Sorry, I didn't know you were coming and I thought it was the best way for Brady to feel the movement of the horse when going into a trot." He smiled. "Then the kid here decided he wanted to go faster."

"Yeah, Mom, I like to go fast."

Jess couldn't take her eyes off the two. Brady was seated in front of Johnny, those big arms framing him protectively. She never doubted that she could trust him to take care of her son, but seeing them together, and the tenderness Johnny showed the boy, still caught her off guard. It made her realize the void that had been in her child's life…and in hers.

A short time later, they were back in the barn. Johnny could see that Brady was tired, too tired to even ask questions. They had a ranch hand take care of Goldie and Beau and Risky, then they all walked out of the barn.

"Jess, could you take Brady back to the house, please? I need to work with Storm."

He saw Jess hesitate, then she asked, "Would you mind if I watched you? I'm sure Nancy will look after Brady. I'd like to see Storm's progress."

"Sure. I'll meet you at the pen."

He watched Jess hurry off with Brady. He knew this had been a good day for the boy. He'd had too many good times with both mother and son and he already knew it was going to be hell to leave here. But he would have to go sooner or later.

He walked to Storm's stall. The animal was a lot calmer these days, and there was trust building between them. The stallion might let Johnny be around him, but at the moment he wasn't sure who else Storm trusted.

He thought maybe Randy could work him, and the more he thought about it, the more it seemed like a good idea. He trusted Randy. And before he left the ranch, he needed to know that the horse would be in good hands. He walked in and Storm didn't flinch. A good sign. "Hey, boy. How do you feel about showing off today?"

The horse came up to him and Johnny rubbed his forehead, then stroked his gloved hands over Storm's back and hindquarters. There were still parts of the animal's body where he didn't like being touched, but the kicking had stopped. Johnny snapped on the lead rope, but left it slack, and the horse followed him out of the stall and outside into the pen. He found Jess waiting for him.

Randy was also there with a long flexible stick with a red bandanna attached to its end. He wanted to saddle Storm today. He'd been putting it off, but it was time.

Once inside the pen, Jess came to the railing. "Oh, my, what a difference there is in him."

"Storm puts up with me, but I'm not sure about anyone else. Randy has helped me sometimes. But there are days that he can't get near the horse. And to be honest, we need to make some decisions about Storm."

"There are no decisions for me, Johnny. You have control of Storm. My dad trusted you, so I trust you."

Her words meant a lot to him. Johnny nodded, then put Storm through his routine. Using the pole with the flag, he rubbed it over the horse, concentrating on the back of his legs where he'd been whipped, letting the animal know that touch didn't always mean being hurt.

Jess watched in amazement as Johnny worked the horse. There was an obvious bond forming between the two, and trust as he touched and stroked the large animal. When Johnny turned his back and walked away, the horse followed him like a puppy. There wasn't any resemblance to the rough stallion from a month ago.

Jess noticed that several of the ranch hands had gathered around the pen as Johnny came to the gate and took a horse blanket from Randy.

She held her breath as Johnny talked softly to Storm, soothing him, gently stroking him as he introduced the animal to the blanket. When Storm didn't move, he slipped on the saddle. That didn't go as well, and Johnny removed it, then began talking gently as he stroked the animal's back until he finally calmed down. Again, he raised the saddle and gently placed it on his back and managed to tighten the cinch. Storm twitched a few times but he stood still.

Then Johnny took the lead rope and walked out of the pen. He stopped beside Jess. "I need more room."

"Are you going to ride him?"

"I'm not, but Randy is."

She was left with her mouth open when Wes came up to her. "He knows what he's doing, Jess. We need to trust him."

She did. "That still doesn't stop me from worrying."

Wes grinned. "Come on, Jess, I don't want to miss this."

They walked over to the bigger corral and climbed up on the railing. The men knew to keep quiet so as not to spook the horse. Johnny had Randy with him, giving him instructions on how to touch and stroke Storm. The horse didn't seem to mind him. Of course, Jess knew that no one but Clay had been on Storm since the horse was brought to the ranch two years ago.

Johnny walked over to where Risky had been brought out and tied to the post. He took the lariat off the saddle horn and made a large loop, then placed it on the ground close to Storm's back right hoof. Randy tugged on Storm to take a step forward and Johnny tightened the rope just between the hoof and heel. He walked back to his mount and climbed on.

"Okay, Randy, cowboy up."

The young stablehand nodded, then approached the horse and it seemed everyone held their breath as he put his foot in the stirrup and swung his leg over Storm's back. The stallion immediately danced around and

whinnied, but was quickly stopped as Johnny tightened the rope, pulling the hind leg up.

Johnny then instructed Randy to get Storm to canter. The horse began to circle the arena, but then he
tried to buck Randy off. Another jerk on the rope and
Storm stopped bucking. The routine went on for the
next twenty minutes until the large black stallion was
loping around the arena in a smooth three-beat gait.

Johnny finally told Randy to stop the horse and dis-
mount. Then Johnny removed the rope and he climbed
on Storm. He sat on the animal as if man and horse
belonged together. Johnny held the reins, but the commands were relayed to the horse by leg pressure only.

Johnny turned Storm left, then right, then he re-
versed the graceful movements. The routine went on
like a ballet and excited murmurs went through the men
watching the performance. Jess finally saw Johnny
smile. He leaned down and rubbed Storm as he spoke
to him. Finally he climbed off and hugged the animal's neck.

Jess's eyes filled as she looked heavenward and
whispered, "You see him, Dad? Storm is everything
you hoped he'd be."

Johnny felt the emotions surface. It always happened
when he reached a breakthrough, when a horse finally
trusted him. He knew it was the meeting of minds and
hearts when they reached an understanding. Like this
horse, Johnny knew what it was like to be physically
beaten. To have someone try to break your spirit, to
destroy your soul. He'd lived through it when he was
growing up. He'd fought back until he had to run away.
It was hard to trust after everyone had let you down.

He rubbed the horse. Funny, he'd always trusted animals more than humans.

"You made it, Storm," he whispered against the horse's neck. "You're free. No one will hurt you again." The horse bobbed his head up and down and let out a whinny.

Johnny smiled and saw Jess coming toward him and his gut tightened in need. He wanted to trust her more than anything. He wanted to reach out and share his feelings with her, his hopes and dreams. Still he held back. He found it easier to share his body than his soul. Yet, all his fears couldn't stop him from wanting her.

Jess was hesitant as she said, "If it's okay, can I pet Storm?"

Johnny nodded. "I don't want crowds around him, but he's used to you."

Jess went right to Storm. He liked that she was so comfortable around him.

"Hey, big guy. I've missed you."

Storm nuzzled her and she laughed. Johnny's heart swelled in his chest. He didn't think he could want her more, but watching her enjoy this animal only added to her appeal. She was a natural.

And he was a goner.

CHAPTER NINE

By NINE o'clock that night, Jess had Brady tucked into bed at the ranch with Nancy watching him overnight and the next morning.

After the day's excitement with Storm, Jess wasn't ready to go home to a lonely apartment. And Johnny had disappeared. That was why she got talked into meeting Molly for ladies' night at the Saddle Up Bar and Grill.

She made a quick stop at home to freshen up. She brushed out her hair and put on nice jeans and a black turtleneck sweater.

Ten minutes later, she pulled into the bar's parking lot. She saw Molly's car and walked over as her friend got out.

Molly was dressed in jeans and a blouse covered by a brown leather jacket. "You look good."

"Do I?" Jess was having second thoughts. "I'm not sure this is a good idea."

"You always say that. All we're doing is going out for a few drinks." She grabbed Jess's arm and headed for the door. "Besides, you need to get out more. And never, ever sit around and wait for a man to call."

Even before they got inside, the music hit them. The

bar area was crowded with both men and women. Molly pointed to a group of her friends and they cut through the tables to an end booth.

"Hey, Maria and Bonnie, you remember Jess."

The music was so loud that she could barely hear the introductions, but remembered them from school. The waitress appeared and Molly ordered a pitcher of beer as they sat down in the booth. Before she knew what happened, a man came by and coaxed her onto the small dance floor for a lively two-step.

Two dances later with an enthusiastic partner, Jess wasn't sure what she wanted tonight, but so far this wasn't it.

Somehow Johnny ended up going into town with some of the crew. They were all still jazzed about Storm. He guessed he was, too, but he'd have been better off just going to bed early.

Instead, he was headed into the Saddle Up. The group went straight to the bar. Randy ordered a beer and asked him what he wanted. The kid wanted to buy him a round. Johnny let him.

He reached for the long neck and took a hearty drink. It tasted good. He usually didn't indulge in alcohol while on the job, but after today's breakthrough Storm's training was nearly complete.

Randy nudged him. "Hey, what do know, Jess is here."

Johnny swung around to see for himself. He spotted her on the dance floor. She was wearing a fitted sweater and a pair of tight jeans that should be illegal. He watched as her body moved seductively to the music. He didn't know the guy who was her partner, but found he didn't like to see his hands on her.

"Hey, cowboy."

He turned to see Molly had walked up to the bar. "Hey, Molly," he said, raising his voice so she could hear him over the music. "What are you doing here?"

She winked at him. "Just lookin' for a little fun, maybe a little trouble."

He nodded toward the dance floor. "You talk Jess into coming tonight?"

She shrugged. "She said she wanted to go out." She eyed him closely. "It's good for her to go out once in a while. Most of the single guys in town have always wanted a chance with her. She was never interested." Molly glanced over her shoulder at her friend. "Looks like she decided to give Rusty a dance." She took a drink of her beer. "I'd say he isn't going to waste a minute it."

Johnny tensed, hating that another man had his hands on her. "I can't control who Jess dances with."

Molly studied him for a moment. "I've been friends with her since first grade. She's the kindest person I know and naive when it comes to men."

"I doubt Jess is going to do something she doesn't want to do."

She shrugged. "Sometimes the loneliness gets to be too much, especially when you can't have what you truly want," she said, then walked away.

Johnny knew the feeling. He looked back at Jess and felt a tightening in his chest. Yeah, he wanted to be with her. So much it scared the hell out of him. That alone should keep him away, but it didn't. He put the beer bottle on the counter and crossed the crowded room to her.

Jess was tired. How did Molly do this all the time? She didn't like dancing with so many different men. All right, she knew most of them from school or town. But that didn't mean she wanted to get jerked, pulled and even groped. Finally the music ended and she was starting off the floor to tell Molly she was going to leave.

She felt a hand on her arm and turned to see the man who'd been causing her restlessness, and her lack of sleep. She blinked in surprise. "Johnny. What are you doing here?"

He took her hand. "I could ask you the same thing." He drew her into his arms as a ballad began to play from the DJ booth. It was George Strait, but she didn't know the name of the song. "I thought you didn't go in for this sort of thing."

She felt a rush as she leaned into Johnny. "I only wanted to get out for a while." She raised her head. "What about you?"

"The guys wanted to buy me a drink to celebrate what happened with Storm."

She smiled. "Yeah, it was pretty amazing."

"I still need to work with him. And I might suggest that you geld him."

She shook her head. "Now, that's something you need to discuss with Holt."

He nodded. "Later. Right now, I have other things on my mind." He pulled her close.

Jess rested her head against his shoulder as she moved to the gentle rhythm of the song. Johnny's hands moved over her back, pressing her closer to him. She could feel every hard angle of the man, causing a stirring in her body. The man lit a fire and she was burning up.

An hour later, Johnny found himself climbing the steps to Jess's apartment. Earlier he'd watched her leave the bar, get into her car and drive off. Something tore at him as he'd started to head back to the ranch, but soon found himself turning around toward town. God knows he'd tried, but he couldn't stay away from her any longer.

He stood on the small porch landing and released a breath into the cold night, then raised his hand and knocked on the door. The wait seemed endless until he finally heard, "Who is it?"

"Johnny."

There was another long pause, then finally the door opened.

Her gaze locked on his, making his heart race. He knew he should turn around and walk down those steps. He couldn't. Jess Calhoun was more special to him than even he wanted to admit. He had to show her.

He swept her up against him and covered her mouth with his. It was like coming home. Her arms wrapped around him, her scent engulfed him like a familiar blanket. His mouth slanted over hers and parted her lips to taste her, the desire was overwhelming and was quickly becoming addicted. He finally tore his mouth away, and closed the door, then went back to her and rained kisses along her cheek and jaw.

"I want you, Jess Calhoun, don't ever doubt that."

His mouth captured her moan as he lifted her off the floor and walked into the living room. They were both breathless by the time he set her down.

"I want you, too." She pulled him back into another kiss.

He groaned and cupped her face in his hands. "Hey, we got all night."

Johnny liked her eagerness, but still was concerned. "Look, Jess. The last thing I want is for you to have regrets."

"No, it's not that. I want you, too, Johnny. It's just…" She glanced away. "It's just I haven't really been with anyone…for a very long time. I might not know how to please you."

He smiled. "Darlin', you already do so much to me that I've been half-crazy since meeting you."

She released a breath. "I'm glad." She slid off his jacket, tossed it on the sofa and did the same with his hat.

Then she took him by the hand and led him into her bedroom. "I guess you're going to have to show me what I've been missing."

Johnny felt his hands shake. He wanted to show her so much, make her feel everything and erase every rotten thought about the last man in her life.

He kissed her several times, then pulled her sweater off over her head. He touched her wild curls. "I love your hair down."

She smiled. "I'm glad."

"There are so many things I like about you. Maybe I'll get the chance to show you tonight." His hands moved from her face down her slender neck. He felt the goose bumps along her skin as he reached the crest of her full breasts. He lowered his mouth to them. She gasped and her hands moved to his hair, holding him close.

"Oh, Johnny," she breathed.

His eagerness grew and he guided her to the bed. All regret flew out of his head. He wanted to steal this piece of heaven in Jess's arms.

Their night together was filled with the sweetest loving he'd ever known. He wanted to show Jess pleasure and in return it gave him more than he ever thought possible. She took him to places that went beyond the physical. Just having her in his arms and holding her gave him the peace he'd never known before. But the hours quickly slipped away and the dawn would soon invade their world.

"Jess." Johnny snuggled up behind her in bed. It was still dark outside, but he needed to get back to the ranch. Mainly he didn't want the employees to see his truck parked next to hers.

"Jess," he whispered, and drew her closer. God, he didn't want to leave her.

She moaned and rolled over. "Johnny? Is it time to get up?"

"No, but I should get back to the ranch. And I don't know when the workers start at the bakery."

She raised her head, and brushed back that gorgeous blond hair of hers. He shivered, recalling the feel of the silken strands against his body.

"We have time," she told him as she glanced at the alarm clock. She leaned forward and kissed him, slow and easy, at the same time moving her luscious body against his.

She pulled back slightly. "Maybe you have some time for a little more instruction."

He laughed. "I've created a monster." When they'd made love the first time, she'd been shy and he loved being able to give her pleasure. And she learned quickly to give it back to him in return. That could be dangerous. If he didn't stop soon, he might never.

All the argument went out of him when she looked at him with those big eyes, her lips full and inviting. His gut tightened with need. A need for this woman. He was afraid that feeling would never go away.

He placed his hand around the back of her neck and lowered his mouth to hers. "I guess I can stay another thirty minutes if my boss doesn't care."

"Not if you give her some of your special attention."

"Yes, ma'am." He covered her mouth, already knowing there wasn't enough time in the world to show Jess everything he wanted to show her.

At 6:30 a.m., Jess hurried downstairs to the bakery. She felt heat rush to her face as she came through the back door and found Carol and Molly already busy at work in the kitchen.

She wasn't late exactly so why did she feel guilty? Not to mention a little giddy. It was surprising what a little loving could do for her disposition.

She recalled last night with Johnny. He'd made love to her twice, showing her all the things that she'd missed in never having a real relationship. She and

Chad had been groping kids compared to how Johnny made her feel.

This morning, he was gone when she woke, but he'd left a sweet note.

"If I woke you, I would never leave. See you later. J."

She tried to hide her smile as she tied on her apron, but Molly was wise to her. "What's going on with you today?" her friend asked. "If I didn't know any better I'd say you got lucky last night. I'll bet it was with Johnny, wasn't it?"

Jess froze and Molly caught the hesitation. Her friend grabbed her by the arm and walked her into the front of the store. It was empty and they could have some privacy.

"Spill it," her friend said. "Who put the smile on your face?"

"I don't kiss and tell."

"That's only because you never have anything to tell." Molly folded her arms and waited. "Don't make me hurt you." She got a strange look on her face, then said, "Johnny. It was Johnny, wasn't it? I talked to him at the bar and you danced with him, and you were out to dinner with him the other night."

"Yes, it was Johnny."

"Damn. I'm jealous." Molly raised a hand. "Not the way you think. Just tell me he treated you good."

"Oh, Molly, I never knew it could be this way."

"Okay, that morning-after glow will wear off soon. I just don't want you to get hurt. He'll be leaving, Jess."

She didn't want to think about that. Not now. "I know. And I don't expect anything from him."

Molly didn't look convinced. "You're not the type

to jump into bed with a guy unless you're half in love with him."

Jess tried to hide any emotion but it was useless with her friend. "Can't you just be happy for me?"

Molly hugged her. "Oh, darlin', that goes without saying. I just hope Johnny Jameson knows what a lucky guy he is."

"Hey, Johnny!" Brady called to him. "Look!"

Johnny had been watching for the past hour. "I can see you," he called to the boy on the back of his pony. They'd been working the past hour, but the boy showed no signs of wanting to quit. He had to smile watching Brady with Beau. The two had become good friends in the past week.

Using the commands that Johnny had taught him, Brady trotted toward him, then stopped the pony right outside the barn. "Was that good?"

"You did great!" He patted the horse. "You can't do it much better than that."

The boy grinned. "Now can I go see Storm?"

Johnny was taken aback by the boy's determination. They'd spent about an hour this morning with Wes, and two sheep, trying to show Brady how to ride for the Mutton Bustin' event. And after lunch, he came back out to take a riding lesson on Beau. All the time he kept asking about Storm.

"I'm not sure your mother would like that."

"Why? You fixed Storm. He's not mean anymore."

"I know, but you're still a kid. I'm not the boss of you."

The boy watched him a moment. "You mean like being my dad?"

That froze him in his tracks. He wasn't sure how to answer that one. "That means, I'm not your parent and there's no one else around. We could go to his stall and see him. I want to make sure he gets used to you being around."

"Oh, boy." Brady swung his leg over the back of Beau. Johnny helped him reach the ground. Together they put the pony back in his stall. Johnny had showed the boy how to take care of the horse. Although the saddle was too heavy, the child helped muck out his stall and brush the animal.

After the gate was closed, they walked toward the back of the barn where Storm's stall was located. Brady slowed.

"You don't have to do this, son," Johnny told him.

"But I want to pet him. I want to be Storm's friend." He raised his arms. "Will you hold me up?"

"Sure." Johnny lifted the boy and settled him on his arm. They went the rest of the way to the enclosed stall. Johnny opened the top door and swung it open. The black horse immediately came over.

Johnny stood back as to not frighten the boy. "Hey, Storm. I brought someone who wants to meet you. Storm, this is Brady Calhoun. Brady meet Night Storm."

The child laughed as the horse whinnied and bobbed his head up and down. Keeping his body between the animal and boy, Johnny stroked the horse. "See, he wants to be friendly. Horses like other horses and people around them."

"Hi, Storm. Grandpa loved you the best of all his horses." Johnny was surprised when the small hand reached out and touched Storm's face. The animal stood perfectly still, allowing it.

Brady gave one of his sweet smiles. "He likes me."

"He does. He knows now you won't hurt him. He's starting to trust people. Sometimes that's hard to do, especially when people hurt you."

Brady leaned toward the horse, causing Johnny to take a step closer. The boy eagerly placed his arms around Storm's neck. "I won't hurt you, Storm. Johnny and Mom, Wes and Uncle Holt won't let anybody hurt you ever."

Johnny felt his heart tighten as he watched the two begin to bond, starting to build a trust and friendship. It was incredible to see, the big horse and the little boy.

Johnny turned and saw Jess watching them. There were tears in her eyes, but she was smiling.

"Mom," Brady said. "Look, I'm touching Storm. He's soft like Beau. And he doesn't want to hurt me." The horse blew air out of his nostrils and shook his head.

Jess was still choked on her emotions from seeing this beloved horse with her son. "Storm is a sweetie." She came up and stroked the animal, too. "Johnny did a wonderful job with him."

They were all clustered around the horse. So close, Jess could feel the man's heat. She inhaled the scent that was pure Johnny.

"He just needed to know we weren't going to hurt him," Johnny said as he eyed her closely. It reminded her of last night when his gaze combed over her body. She shivered as if feeling his touch.

"Are you going to kiss Mom?"

Jess felt the heat rise to her face. Johnny smiled, then leaned down. "She's so pretty I think I will." He placed a sweet kiss on her lips.

That satisfied her son, but not her. She turned to Brady. "What are you two doing here? I thought you were learning to ride Beau."

"I already did that. I want to watch Johnny ride Storm."

"I needed to make sure it was okay with you before he's around the horse," Johnny told her.

"I'm not comfortable with Brady in the corral yet, but I don't have a problem with him watching you work him. I'd like to watch, too."

Johnny set Brady down. "Of course. Storm needs to be around people. He did fine this morning with Randy and Wes." He had trouble concentrating on what he was saying. Thoughts of last night and this beautiful woman kept distracting him. He glanced at the horse. He was in big trouble if he couldn't concentrate on his job.

Fifteen minutes later, Johnny walked Storm out of the barn. More like the saddled horse followed him into the corral. That was how Johnny liked it. When trust was finally formed between him and the horse. That meant that his job was nearly finished.

Johnny knew that he wasn't going to be needed here much longer. Randy and Wes knew his technique well enough to train the dozen other horses that resided at the Double Bar C.

He'd already been approached by a few ranchers in the area to run a clinic to help with other problem horses. Johnny still wasn't sure if that was a good idea. When he left this place, he needed to make a clean break.

He glanced at Jess and Brady sitting on the railing waiting for him. That was what he couldn't handle. He didn't want people to have expectations of him. He was good with horses, not people. Next week was the Little Buckaroo Rodeo. That had to be his deadline. He had to leave then, especially after spending the night with Jess in his arms.

Jess saw Johnny climb onto Storm's back. A thrill shot through her as she realized she was in love with this man. There was nothing about him that she didn't like. His way with animals, her son and with her. She sighed. Last night, he'd showed her his gentleness when he'd made love to her. He was a special man.

She watched him run Storm through a routine of commands. It still amazed her, the gentle power he possessed on horseback. She couldn't help but wonder about the kid he'd been. She knew his mother hadn't seemed to care about him. His father he couldn't find.

She so admired the wonderful man he'd turned out to be. That was the man she didn't want to give up, and she would fight to keep him.

CHAPTER TEN

THAT evening Johnny paced around his apartment, thinking seriously about driving into town for a strong drink. If not, he might end up back at the ranch house with Jess.

He'd barely made it through supper with her sitting across the table. He should have gotten up and left, but he told himself he needed to be cordial. The truth was he didn't want to leave Jess at all.

Okay, that right there meant trouble for him. That meant he was getting too close.

When she went upstairs to put Brady down for the night that was when he'd left. He had to stop putting himself in positions that made him think he could be a part of a family. He'd tried it once and it hadn't worked. He doubted it would work with Jess.

There was a soft knock on the door and he went to open it.

Jess stood on the small porch. "Is something wrong?" she asked.

He only shook his head.

Jess's heart was already drumming a fast pace, then she saw Johnny's bare chest and his jeans partly unbuttoned and nearly lost it.

"I'm sorry," she began. "I didn't mean to disturb you. I… Never mind. I'll go."

Before she had a chance to take a step, Johnny reached for her and pulled her inside, then shut the door. "Why did you come by here, if only to leave?"

She swallowed back the dryness. "To be honest, I wasn't sure if I should. I agreed to no strings."

"That doesn't mean you're not welcome. Although I'm not crazy about everyone knowing what goes on in my personal life."

"You mean the ranch hands?"

He nodded. "It's for your protection, Jess. Your reputation."

She couldn't help but smile. "Johnny, I've survived a lot worse."

"You deserve better."

He walked to the sofa and pulled on a T-shirt. She wanted to object when he covered his toned chest. The memories of her touching his heated skin, feeling the defined muscles, flashed in her head.

Johnny didn't want Jess sneaking around at night as if she were doing something wrong. He didn't want her to be the cause of gossip after he left town.

"I don't like you talking about yourself that way."

"Look, Jess. You're a Calhoun and part of this community. Your family has been in this area for generations. It isn't the same for me. I couldn't tell you about my kin if I wanted to. At the very least their values are in question."

She went to him. "There had to be someone good in your life, Johnny. Someone who cared about you or you wouldn't have turned out to be such a good man."

He ignored the question. "So is there a reason you came by?"

"Cheyenne wanted me to ask you if you'd ride in the opening ceremony for the rodeo."

He frowned. "Why me? It should be a Calhoun who participates around here."

"For one thing, all my siblings are out of town at the moment. And if you wanted to, Johnny, you could be a part of this town," she said. "People would welcome you with open arms."

He glanced away. "Come on, Jess. I told you I like having my truck and trailer, so I can stop and go whenever I want. That's all I need."

"Are you sure?" She took a step closer. "Have you ever had a reason to make a home somewhere? Somewhere where there's family?"

He smiled, but she could see he was masking the pain. "It's been a lot of years since anyone in my family cared where I was."

His silver gaze locked on to hers. "Not all mothers are like you, Jess. Mine would definitely never make Mother of the Year. Not when she chose to stay with the guy who beat her, rather than take her son to safety."

Jess ached to go to him. She wanted to tell him that there were other people who loved him. "Who raised you?"

His expression softened. "I pretty much took care of myself, but Will Nichols was there to knock some sense into me if I needed it." A smile slowly began to appear. "He managed to teach me some table manners and a lot about horses."

Jess relaxed with Johnny opening up to her. "So he's the one who taught you the training skills."

"Yeah. Will was something to see."

"I think you're something, too. I couldn't believe that Storm could be saved. Yet that's what you did, Johnny. You saved him. I know it's crazy, but that horse was such a big part of my father."

"No, it's not crazy," he told her. "The two had a strong bond."

She nodded. "I know one thing, my dad would be very grateful that Storm is doing so well."

"He's getting there…a few more weeks."

She blinked. "That's all?"

Johnny nodded. He knew that he had to tell her. Let her know he would break it off between them when he packed up and left. Warn her before he made it worse, for both of them. He put on a smile. "Isn't that what you wanted, for Storm to get better?"

"Of course it is."

He couldn't help but stare at this beautiful woman. After the night in Jess's bed, he knew he'd crossed the line, and if he wasn't careful he'd never be able to give her up. Right now, he wanted nothing more than to grab her and continue what they started last night. Problem was, wanting Jess Calhoun was something that wasn't going to stop anytime soon.

"I guess I better go." She turned to leave and something inside him ached to have her.

He reached out and took her arm. When she didn't protest, he drew her against him, then his mouth came down on hers. It hadn't been even twenty-four hours since he'd made love to her and he was hungry for her again.

He tore his mouth away. "I've wanted to do that since I left you this morning. All I could think about all day was you." He kissed her again. "How it felt to hold you in my arms. Damn, Jess. I should make you leave, but I can't seem to let you go."

She wrapped her arms around his neck and pulled his head back down. "Then don't."

He closed his eyes, feeling her body pressed against his. He wanted her. "I'm no good for you."

"I believe my father was a good judge of character. He wouldn't have hired you if you weren't a good guy, Johnny Jameson." She kissed him softly. "I've seen you with people and with the horses. I know firsthand your tender touch."

He'd never met a woman like Jess and he was beginning to care too much. But the fact was, he was capable of hurting her. God knew he didn't want to, but he would walk out of her life. He had to. It was all he knew.

"I can't give you what you want, Jess."

Jess had to hold her disappointment in check. She didn't want this man to see how his words hurt her. "Did I ask for anything you couldn't give me?"

He shook his head.

Jess didn't need to ask. Johnny Jameson was everything she wanted in a man. She'd never felt so treasured, so...loved. He had to feel it, too. "And I never will. And if you want me to leave now, I'll go." She had to get out of there before she humiliated herself. She turned around and reached for the doorknob when she felt Johnny's hand on her arm.

"I can't let you go, Jess." He touched her face and made her look at him. "This might be a really bad idea. I can't offer you anything but this. Right now."

She stepped into his embrace. "I told you, Johnny, I'm not asking for anything more," she breathed against his mouth.

His head dipped to hers and he captured her mouth.

She opened to him, giving him as good as she got. Once he tasted her, felt her body against his, heard her little moaning sounds, he was lost.

And from this woman, he might never recover.

The next afternoon, Johnny and Wes worked with Brady to help him learn how to stay on the sheep's back. He had to admit the kid was determined if nothing else.

Several of the ranch hands were watching and cheering the boy on as he gripped the sheep around the neck and hung on for dear life as the animal raced out of the chute.

"That's it, Brady. You ride 'em."

Wes had his stopwatch to check the time. The longest ride had been six seconds. But for a boy turning five years old next week that was pretty good.

Johnny went and helped the boy up. "You did great, son."

"Did I stay on long enough?"

"Almost. But I think we should stop for today."

Johnny went to remove the protective helmet from Brady's head, but the boy backed away. "No, I need to do it again until I get better."

"You are better, Brady," Wes said. "But you're tired

and so are the sheep. You've been at this for over an hour."

The foreman went to gather up the sheep in the corral. He and the men took them back to the pasture.

Johnny could see the boy's tears building and knelt down beside him. "Hey, what's the matter, partner?"

"I hafta get better. Tucker said I'm a baby and he's gonna win the belt buckle. I want to beat him."

"Well, Tucker is wrong. You never know who's gonna win until the day of the rodeo. But the most important thing to remember is that you play fair. Don't be a bad sport. Win or lose, you always have to be polite. Shake hands. Got that?"

Brady nodded. "I want to make Grandpa proud of me."

How did he answer that one? "I only met your grandfather once, but I knew right off Clay Calhoun was a good man. He'd want you to be a good sport, too. A real cowboy, like your grandfather, is honest and truthful and he doesn't cheat."

Brady nodded. "What if Tucker is not very nice to me?"

"You still be nice to him."

The kid wrinkled his nose. "What if I don't want to?"

Johnny had to work to keep from laughing. "Someday you'll be glad you did because that makes you the bigger man."

Brady wiped the hair off his forehead. "And because it's the cowboy way."

"That's right."

The boy grinned and threw himself into Johnny's arms.

Something tightened in Johnny's chest as he felt those tiny arms wrap around his neck. "I'm glad you came to live here," Brady whispered against his cheek.

Johnny found himself cradling the child close. "I'm glad I did, too." He thought of the boy's mother, and knew things would never be the same for him when he left Larkville.

Fighting his emotions, he finally released Brady and stood. "I better go and do my job now."

"Can I watch you work Storm?"

"I'm not sure. That's your mother's decision."

"His mother says it's fine."

They both turned to see Jess standing there dressed in her usual jeans and boots, her hair braided and her straw hat shading her whiskey eyes.

"Mom," Brady said, and ran to her. "I was riding sheep."

"I heard that from Wes."

"And I'm gonna beat Tucker."

"Brady," Johnny warned.

"Well, I'm gonna try. But if I lose, I'm still gonna be nice to him. Now, can I watch Johnny work with Storm?"

She looked up at Johnny and smiled. "If I get to come along, too."

"Sure, Mom. You can come, too." He started tugging her arm. "Can't she, Johnny?"

He found he had trouble speaking and gave a nod. The boy took off in front of them.

Johnny fell into step beside her. "You're home early."

She smiled. "Since I'm the boss, I can take off a little early if I need to. It was a slow day, anyway. And

I didn't want you to have to spend the entire day with a five-year-old."

He moved closer, inhaled that familiar scent and memories from last night flooded into his head. "He's a great kid, but honestly, I'd rather spend time with his mother."

"And Brady's mother wouldn't mind a little time with you."

He smiled. Damn, he shouldn't be this happy. "That could be arranged."

"Is that a promise?" she asked teasingly, then heard Brady calling to them. "Looks like it's going to be a lot later."

The boy ran back to them. "Come on, Mom, Johnny."

"Oh, honey, I forgot." She stopped. "We're going to Aunt Molly's house tonight."

"You mean Grandma Carol and Grandpa Ben's house." The boy looked at Johnny. "They aren't my real my grandma and grandpa, but I got permission to call them that."

"Lucky you."

"Hey, Mom, can Johnny go with us?"

Johnny saw the surprised look on her face, and he rushed on to say, "Brady, that's all right. I have a lot to do tonight."

Jess couldn't hide her disappointment. "Anything that can't wait for another evening? The Daytons would love to have you. They've been wanting to meet you."

"Yeah, Johnny," Brady said. "You gotta go, it's homemade pizza. And we get to help."

She smiled. "Yeah, Johnny. This is the time to get

to know some people in town. And Carol and Ben are some of the best."

"Oh, boy," Brady cheered. "It's gonna be so much fun." The child took off toward the house to get cleaned up.

Jess turned to Johnny. "Oh, boy, it's going to be so much fun."

He grabbed her close, not caring who saw them. "I guarantee it's not going to be as much fun as last night." His mouth captured hers. He didn't seem to care about much else except being with Jess.

And that wasn't good, but at the moment he didn't care.

The Dayton family household was loud and filled with laughter. Molly had two younger brothers, Chase and Tyler, and when the three were together, it was chaos. Jess loved being a part of it.

They didn't live in the big old farmhouse where Molly had been raised anymore, but the rental house in town was just as warm and inviting. Carol, with Brady's help, had made three large pizzas with numerous toppings.

The best part was that Johnny fit right in with her friends. Besides her family, the Daytons were the people who meant the most to her. Jess knew it was wishful thinking that Johnny would stay in Larkville and be a part of her life but that hadn't stopped her from dreaming of a future with the man. A father for Brady. Every time she'd seen Johnny with her son she couldn't help but think of being a family. He'd been so understanding and so wonderful with her child. How could she not love him?

"I don't like Johnny anymore," Molly said as she came up to her. "He's siding with my brothers."

Jess smiled. "All men side with your brothers. You just let them get to you."

Molly turned to her. "You got it bad for him, don't you?"

"I could lie and say no, but I'm trying to keep it casual."

"Jessica Calhoun, you don't do casual." There was a long silence, then Molly said, "Does he know you're in love with him?"

Jess could act surprised, but Molly knew her too well. "No, and he probably never will. He's leaving in a few weeks."

Her friend shook her head. "Why is it that we can't keep guys around? I mean, we're great-looking and smart. Ah, maybe that's it. We should play dumb and we could get a man."

Jess didn't want just any man, she wanted Johnny Jameson. He'd been honest from the beginning, and hadn't fed her any promises. She knew where she stood. Too bad that didn't ease the pain.

Johnny looked across the big kitchen at Jess. He found he didn't like being so far away from her. He enjoyed her company.

"Those girls are pretty special to me."

Johnny turned to find Ben Dayton. The older man in his fifties had thinning gray hair and an easy smile.

"They've been inseparable since they met in kindergarten," Ben went on to say. "I couldn't love Jess any more if she were my own."

"I can see how you'd feel that way."

The older man studied him. "And I can tell you care about both Jess and the boy. I'm glad." Ben leaned back against the counter and took a drink of his beer. "She had it pretty rough for a while. As nice as this town is, some people weren't very kind during her pregnancy. Clay protected her as best he could." There was a big grin. "And you don't want to tick off a man like Clay. Some people in this town are sorry they did." Ben shook his head. "Nope, you don't mess with a Calhoun."

"I take it you were friends with Clay?"

Ben nodded. "We'd known each other since school, along with Gus Everett. You might have met him already. He owns the gas station."

"Yeah, I've seen him a few times."

Ben sighed. "Gus and I still miss our poker buddy. It's not the same without Clay. That damn stubbornness of his ended his life far too soon." The man's features softened. "I'm glad you got to meet him. He was a good man. One of the best. Everyone loved him, and they're plannin' to honor him with a big celebration at the fall festival this coming October."

Johnny couldn't help but think how lucky Jess was. "He was a lucky man to have so much family."

Ben smiled. "Yes, he was. And the thing was, Clay knew it." The older man studied Johnny. "Not all people do. Some can't see what's right in front of them."

CHAPTER ELEVEN

THE rest of the week had gone by fast, and Johnny had spent a lot more time with Jess than he needed to think about. He'd been with her most evenings, and that included Brady, too. People were thinking of them as a couple. A family.

Something he didn't know how to change. The longer he'd stayed, the more intertwined in their lives he'd gotten and the more they would be hurt when he left.

And sooner or later, he had to leave.

He walked Storm out of the barn and into the corral. He mounted the animal and rode around the arena. With the way the stallion's progress kept going forward, he knew his days here were numbered. He'd already been getting calls from a potential client, Ted Ransen, from Ransen Stables in Florida.

He'd get a substantial bonus if he could get there in a week. But money wasn't the draw for Johnny. He didn't have the Calhoun wealth, but he'd invested wisely over the years. Enough so he didn't have to worry about going broke. If he took the job, that meant he had to leave for the sunshine state soon. He still had to think about it.

He shook away the thought. "How about a run,

fella?" He rubbed Storm's neck and started out of the corral. Randy opened the gate and they took off through the pasture. The canter quickly changed into a gallop over the open fields.

Johnny leaned down close to the horse's neck. "That's it, boy, run for it. You've earned it." The animal's long graceful strides took them over the field and across the stream.

Johnny smiled. No wonder Clay had wanted this animal—he was magnificent. And the way things were going this horse should sire beautiful, spirited foals.

He circled around and brought the horse back. He slowed at the creek, then came to a stop and climbed off. He let the horse get a drink of water.

Over the past three and a half weeks he'd become attached to this stallion.

"You're such a good boy." He stroked the shiny black coat. "You miss your old buddy, huh? Well, I know a little boy who can't wait to step into the job as your friend." He would miss this magnificent animal, too.

Storm bobbed his head and Johnny climbed back on and wheeled the horse around. "Come on, fella, we better head back home." It struck him how easily he spoke that word.

A sense of comfort overtook him as he thought about the big old house, the people who filled it. The men he worked with at the Double Bar C. His chest tightened with familiar longing. Deep down he'd always wanted a place where he felt he could belong. But he learned a long time ago that just because he wanted something didn't mean he got it.

* * *

Jess had seen Johnny take off on Storm about thirty minutes ago and he hadn't returned. This was the first time the horse had been out of the corral since the day he'd run off.

She was a little worried.

What if Johnny had gotten thrown? He could be out there hurt. She started for the barn to saddle up Goldie when she saw the rider and horse coming over the rise.

She had to stop and watch. The man and animal were a sight to see. They were so in sync in their movements. So graceful it took her breath away. Johnny slowed as they reached the corral and she went to him as he dismounted.

"Hey, I didn't realize you were headed out."

Johnny walked the lathered horse toward the barn. "It was a last-minute decision."

"I was worried. I mean, Storm hasn't been out of the corral."

Johnny gave her a sideways glance as he took the reins and walked toward the barn. "I thought you hired me because of my expertise. I know when a horse is ready. In fact, Storm is past ready."

"He is?"

He stopped and turned to her. "Come on, Jess. We both have seen how well behaved Storm is around people now. The only decision you and Holt have left is if you're going to keep him as a stud."

She was a little hurt by his distant manner. "I'm not going to make that decision until my brother returns."

Johnny shook his head. "You keep saying that, but this ranch is partly yours. You care about this horse. He'd been abused, Jess. Gelding him would naturally make him calmer." He shrugged. "You could wait a year or so, long enough to sire a foal or two to continue the bloodline."

This was the last thing she wanted to talk about with Johnny.

"I'll speak to your brother if you want," Johnny said. "I see how attached Brady is to Storm, and for the future, a gelded horse would be a much better mount for the boy."

"I agree." She finally smiled. She liked how well he fit into her life.

Jess watched as Johnny led the stallion into the barn. Was he trying to put space between them? She felt an urge to run after him and try to convince him how good they were together. But she knew she couldn't do it. Even though she knew Johnny Jameson would leave, that didn't mean she had to be happy about it.

Johnny sat at the big kitchen table enjoying the warmth of the roaring fire and Nancy's meat loaf. He knew he had to cherish these memories and enjoy his time left here. Brady entertained them with silly things. Tonight, though, Johnny couldn't get comfortable in the cozy setting.

He glanced at Jess, who was watching him. She probably could see his restlessness. He *was* feeling restless; he wanted to make it to the rodeo in a few days, then he'd decide it would be time to move on.

The meal had concluded, and Johnny planned a quick good-night before he went back to his place. Then Brady asked him to carry him upstairs to bed. He couldn't deny the boy.

"You excited about Saturday?" Johnny asked.

A pajamas-clad Brady lay back against the pillow. Jess had already gone downstairs, so it was just the two of them. "I don't know."

Johnny sat down on the mattress. "Hey, what's up, kid?"

"Tucker Carson keeps saying I'm not gonna win."

Tucker was doing a job on Brady. "I think Tucker is the one who's worried about the competition."

The boy wrinkled his nose. "What competition?"

"You. Tucker is worried you're so good you'll beat him. He's trying to make you worry, and that's not play-ing fair. So you go out there and try your best. That's all you can do. Win or lose, you give it your all."

Brady grinned. "I can try really hard. Thanks, Johnny." He hugged him. "I love you."

The words froze Johnny on the spot, but then he re-alized he was feeling the same way about the kid. "I care about you, too, Brady."

The boy pulled back and looked him in the eye. "You know what I wish? I wish you were my dad."

Two minutes later, Johnny nearly ran from the house as the boy's words echoed in his head. Once outside, he drew the cold air into his lungs, but the tightness in his chest didn't ease as he walked to the barn.

Love. No, he couldn't do love. He'd tried it before and it hadn't worked. He would only hurt Jess when he messed up. She'd already settled for one louse in her life, she didn't need another man running out on her. He cared about her too much for that.

Damn. He rubbed his hand over his face.

He reached Storm's stall. The top part of the gate had been left open so the stallion could be more social with the other horses. Funny, this was where Johnny felt most comfortable. He always had. Horses hadn't rejected him like people. Animals accepted him with all his moods and faults. He walked up to Storm and he was greeted with a friendly nuzzle.

"Hey, buddy." He stroked the beautiful animal. "I'm going to miss you."

The horse blew a long breath through his nostrils.

Johnny smiled. He wished everything was this simple. He heard his name and turned to see Jess.

She didn't look happy. "Is there a reason you left so quickly?"

He didn't want to look at her. She made him ache for the things he wanted but couldn't have. A place to belong, to fit in.

"I was tired. And I got a phone call I had to return." That was a lie. He'd taken care of the call earlier.

She didn't look convinced. "Johnny, you don't have to sneak off to get time by yourself."

He glanced away. "It's not that, Jess." He knew he had to face her. He owed her that much. "I see Brady getting more and more attached. And I can't give him what he needs."

"You seem to be doing pretty well, so far." She came up to the stall and Storm moved to get attention from her. She stroked the large animal as if he were a big puppy. "Give us a chance, Johnny."

She was killing him. "I don't know how, Jess." He stood back. "I've tried it before. I thought I could settle down with someone, be part of a family." He paused.

"In the end I broke it off, but I still hurt her. I hurt someone who was special to me. Don't you see, I can't do that to you or to Brady."

Jess refused to cry, but the hurt was almost unbearable. She was losing Johnny, but did she really ever have him? Her mind flashed back to nearly six years ago when Chad took off because he couldn't handle parenthood, and didn't love her enough to stay. Even though she knew that had been coming, this was worse. She was in love with Johnny.

She drew a shaky breath and dug her hands into the pockets of her coat. She'd survived those heartaches and she'd survive this.

Johnny reached out to touch her cheek. "Jess, I wish I could give you what you want."

She stepped back. There was no way she would fall apart. "Hey, I can't say you didn't warn me." She cleared her throat and managed a smile. She would get through this. "When? When are you leaving?"

Those gray eyes locked on to hers. "Tomorrow."

She drew in a breath, feeling the sharp pain in her chest. She held her head high, just as her father taught her. "I'll have your check ready."

"Jess, I wish it could be different."

She raised a hand. "Please, Johnny, don't say what you don't mean."

He nodded, then said, "Goodbye, Jess."

Her gaze met his. She felt the intensity clear to her soul; the hurt went just as deep. It took everything in her to speak. "Goodbye, Johnny."

She turned and walked out of the barn before she burst into tears. By the time she reached the house all that was left was a big hole in her heart. As she went upstairs and looked in on her son, the tears started. She could handle the hurt, but damn, Brady wouldn't be able to. Her son didn't deserve this. The worst part was that she knew Johnny Jameson loved them as much as they loved him. Most of all, he needed them.

Early the next morning, it only took about thirty minutes for Johnny to pack up his life into his duffel bags and put them in his truck. The only thing he needed to do was load up Risky. He wanted to be on the road before he had to face anyone, but he wasn't that big a louse. He needed to say goodbye to Brady. He had to find the words, somehow.

He headed for the house in time to see the boy coming out the door. Jess wasn't far behind. His heart was tight as he made his way up the drive.

"Hey, Johnny. Are you ready for practice?"

The boy stopped in front of him. "Sorry, son, not today." Johnny knelt down, finding he was a little shaky. "I have to leave."

"For the day?"

He hated this. "No, I'm afraid not. Since Storm is better, I have to go to another job."

"At another ranch near here?"

Johnny released a breath. "No, it's in Florida."

"Is that in Texas?"

"No, it's a few days' ride from here."

Brady's smiled dropped. "But what about the rodeo? You're still going to help me. You promised."

He gripped the boy's arms. "I'm sorry, son. I can't."

Brady jerked away. "No, don't call me that. You're not my dad. And you broke a promise."

"It can't be helped. You want me to help this horse, don't you?"

He shook his head, fighting tears. "No, I never want you to go away."

Pain slashed through him. "Sometimes it can't be helped."

Brady swiped at the tears on his face. "You said if you promised somebody something, it isn't right not to do it." He was crying now. "You said it's not the cowboy way."

Johnny stood. He had to get out of here. "I wish I could make it different, Brady."

"I don't believe you anymore." The boy ran to his mother. At least he had a mother that was there for him. Jess looked at him and he had to fight not to go to her.

Then they both went back into the house. When the door shut, the loneliness hit like a slap. He'd been closed so many times before, he should be used to it. But this was worse than any other time. He turned and walked back to the barn to get Risky.

"I thought you were a smart guy," a familiar voice said.

Johnny turned and saw Wes. He ignored his comment. "I took some notes about Storm and left them up in the apartment."

Wes folded his arms. "Why didn't you just sneak out in the middle of the night? It would have saved a lot of people a painful goodbye."

Johnny attached the lead rope on his horse and started out of the stall. "I know you don't care much for me right now. I'm sorry about that." He didn't care much for himself, either. He released a breath. "I have a job to go to. It's a commitment I made in Florida."

"What about your commitment here?" Wes challenged.

He stood up to the foreman. "You aren't satisfied with my work? I thought I did what I was hired to do."

"No complaints about that."

Johnny's chest was so tight he could barely draw air into his lungs. "Spit it out, Wes."

"You had me fooled, Johnny." The foreman shook his head. "I saw how you were with Brady. There was a bond there. And Jess. You know she hadn't given another man a chance since Brady's father, and then you came along." Wes looked him in the eye. "If I thought it would do any good, I'd beat some sense into you. Good Lord, man. Do you have any idea what you're leaving behind?"

They got to the trailer. Hell, yes, he did. That was why he was heading out. "This is my job. I go where the work is. I can't hang around here and sponge off the Calhouns."

Wes took hold of Johnny's arm. "If there was one thing about Clay Calhoun that I want you to leave here knowing, it's that he was a great judge of character. You could have made horses dance, but if Clay didn't think you were a good person, he wouldn't have bothered with you. Just remember, it was Clay who hired you."

Wes pulled a check out of his pocket and handed it to him. "I'm going to say what Clay would say. Thank you, Johnny, and if you ever want it, there's always a place here for you at the Double Bar C."

* * *

That night, Jess stayed at the ranch with Brady. With the rodeo the next day, they needed to load Goldie and Beau into the trailer to get them to the arena for the opening ceremony.

It took a while to get her son asleep. Not because of the excitement of the next day, but because he didn't want to go anymore. Between her and Wes, they managed to convince him to participate if only because he would be the only Calhoun to ride.

She went downstairs and stepped into her father's office. Memories of bedtime kisses and stern discussions about grades and broken curfews flashed into her head. It was still hard to believe he was gone. Clay Calhoun had been a big robust man. He loved his friends and his family. He'd been there so many times for her to count, but not this time.

And she needed him now.

She released a breath and sank down into the desk chair. She had to put Johnny Jameson out of her head. He was gone.

Funny, when Chad had taken off, she'd been almost relieved that he chose not to stay by her. She didn't love him. She hadn't known what love was until she met Johnny.

A knock sounded on the open door. "Hey, Jess. You busy?"

She looked up to see Wes. "No, just missing Dad."

"We all do." Wes walked in and placed the check that she wrote out that morning. "What's this?"

"Johnny wouldn't take it."

"What do you mean? He spent weeks here working with Storm…and Brady."

"Sorry, I tried, but the man refused to take the money. I couldn't very well cram it down his throat. Not saying I wouldn't have wanted to." Wes started to leave and she stopped him.

She swallowed back the tightness in her throat. "What did I do wrong, Wes?"

"Oh, darlin', this has nothing to do with you."

"Then what?"

"Johnny's been on his own for so long, I think he needs to keep going so the loneliness doesn't catch up." Wes nodded. "Trust is a hard thing to come by. I think he's also afraid he'll let you down."

She felt a surge of hope. "What?"

"He doesn't feel that he can live up to what you both need."

"He's everything to me," Jess admitted to him. "And you know how Brady feels about him."

The foreman shook his head. "But Johnny's got to feel it. I never met a man so dead set on running away from belonging."

Johnny's truck was eating up the miles of road, and he hadn't even gotten out of Texas. Yet even concentrating on the long drive, he couldn't get Jess and Brady out of his head.

He hit the steering wheel with his hand. Any man would want that boy for a son, and it nearly broke Johnny's heart when Brady told him to leave. That feeling of rejection was something that Johnny knew all too well.

He'd been rejected enough to know the hurt the kid was going through. It scarred you. It was worse for a kid. No, Brady would be better off without him. The boy would get over his leaving. Wouldn't he?

He remembered back to how he'd leave messages around the honky-tonk circuit for Jake but his old man had never contacted him.

Johnny shook away the memory. He had to close those doors, knowing that it had stopped him from making any kind of life for himself.

Life? This was his life. He lived out of his truck. He'd told himself for so long that this was what he wanted that he'd believed it. But he was still alone, even if he had somewhere to live.

He thought back to his relationship with Amy and his need to move on. Maybe it wasn't settling down that had been the problem as much as that fact that he didn't love her enough.

His feelings were different for Jess. He loved her. The breath caught in his lungs. Oh, God, he did love her, and the boy, too.

It suddenly struck him. He was doing the same thing to Brady that his father had done to him. Running away.

Damn, he'd run out on both of them.

It was all clearing in his head. He wanted it all with Jess—a home, a family, a place to belong.

The sun was high in the sky in front of the truck windshield and that was when he saw the sign, telling him he was entering the state of Louisiana.

No, he didn't want to go there. It struck him—he didn't want to be anywhere but in Larkville, Texas. And with Jess.

CHAPTER TWELVE

TODAY was the First Annual Little Buckaroo Rodeo. Jess was more nervous than if she was the one competing instead of her son. Brady had been quiet during breakfast. He didn't eat much, or say much. She knew she had to leave him alone and let him decide how to handle today.

It tore at her heart when she'd heard him crying last night, and even when she went to him she couldn't help. She didn't ask any questions, only murmured to her son how much she loved him and she'd never leave him. Finally Brady fell asleep. She'd stayed awhile longer, wishing she could find a way to make everything better.

How could she? She felt the guilt of letting a man into her son's life when she knew he wouldn't stay around.

Dear God. She had to forget about Johnny Jameson. He was gone and they had to move on. Maybe today would help, but she knew that she and Brady would get a lot of questions about Johnny's absence. Hey, she'd handled it years ago, she could handle it now. She was a Calhoun.

They'd arrived at the rodeo grounds early and Wes

unloaded Beau and Goldie for the ride in the opening ceremony. She only wished Brady looked happier about it.

"Hey, you look nice in your new shirt and jeans," she told him.

A week ago, they'd gone out and gotten Brady a new burgundy-colored Western shirt with white piping and a black jeans jacket. He wore the black Stetson his grandfather had given him for his past birthday.

She heard her name and turned to see Molly coming toward her. "Hey, there, partner, you look sharp," she told Brady.

"Thanks." The child wandered off toward the trailer.

Molly turned to her. "You better hope I don't run into a certain horse trainer. I won't be held accountable for my actions."

Jess smiled. "You're a good friend, Mol," she said. "What's up?"

"Everything's fine. The booth is up and running and we're selling all the pastries we brought with us. Mom's working it and Dad's headed back to the bakery to get more."

Jess scanned the good-size crowd filing into the covered arena. "Good. At least the school will make money. We'll hold off before we sell the cakes and pie slices."

"If we put it out they'll probably buy it." Molly studied her. "How are you doing?"

She shrugged. "I'm a little cold, but hey, once all the people get here it'll warm up."

"That's not what I'm talking about."

Jess had called her friend late last night and given

her a short synopsis of what had happened with Johnny. "I know, but that's all I want to discuss right now. I'm trying to hold it together for my son. You and I can have a cryfest later."

"I'm sorry that I told you to go for it."

Jess smiled at her best friend. "It's not your fault. I would have fallen for Johnny, anyway."

"I see a girls' night out in your future."

Jess groaned as Molly took off. That was the last thing she needed.

Johnny drove as fast as possible and was relieved when he pulled onto Calhoun property. That soon disappeared when he saw that the ranch compound was deserted. He shouldn't be surprised, as the rodeo was taking place today.

He climbed out as Randy came out of the barn. "Hey, Johnny, what are you doing here? I heard you left for Florida."

"I forgot something." He looked around. "Hey, do you think you can do me a favor?"

The boy frowned. "What?"

"I need you to take Risky out of the trailer. And I need to load Storm into it."

Randy didn't look so sure of the request.

"I'm taking him to the rodeo to ride in the opening ceremony."

The ranch hand grinned. "All right."

Johnny headed into the barn and hurried to Storm's stall. The horse came to the gate and let out a welcoming whinny. "At least someone is glad to see me." The animal nuzzled his hand. "Hey, buddy, you want to go with me to keep a promise to a little boy?"

Ten minutes later Storm was loaded into the trailer, decked out in silver-studded tack. They headed to the rodeo grounds to where Johnny would hopefully have a second chance with Jess. He probably didn't deserve one, but he was going to beg for one if he had to. He drove as fast as was safe. At least Storm was handling the ride. He hoped that his idea worked out, as well.

He arrived at the entrance to the Larkville Corral to see a line of cars and trucks waiting to get in. When his turn came, it was Gus Everett taking the parking fee.

"Well, hello, Johnny," the old guy greeted him. "I thought you'd be here before now."

"Hi, Gus. I got held up so I need to get to the arena before the opening ceremony."

The older man glanced back at the trailer. "Well, I'll be dammed—that looks like Clay's horse?"

"Yep, and he's going to be in the opening ceremony, if I get there."

"You know when you first showed up here, I wasn't sure you could hold your own." The older guy pushed his hat back. "It's not very often I'm wrong about a person, but I was about you. You're the real deal, Johnny Jameson. I hope you decide to hang around town." Gus grinned, then gave him directions to the back of the arena.

Excitement raced through Johnny as he drove over the grassy area. He was going to need help to convince Jess to take another chance on him.

* * *

"No! I don't want to ride," Brady insisted as he backed away from his pony. "I'm afraid."

Jess looked at Wes to catch his shrug. "Since when are you afraid of Beau?" she asked.

"Since now."

"All right, son, if you don't want to ride in the parade you don't have to."

Just then the Carson family—Cheyenne, Derrick and their son, Tucker—rode their horses along the other side of the railing. "Jess, is there a problem?" she asked.

This was the last thing she needed right now. "No. We're fine. Just give us a few minutes."

"Don't take too long. We can't hold up the ceremony much longer," Cheyenne said, and moved her horse along with the rest of the Carsons. Then Tucker turned and stuck his tongue out at Brady.

"Are you going to let him get away with that?" Jess heard a familiar voice say.

She turned around at the same time Brady yelled, "Johnny!"

The child ran up to him. "I thought you had to go to Florida."

Jess tensed as Johnny crouched down in front of her son. "A funny thing happened—I discovered I couldn't leave Texas."

Brady smiled. "So you came back?"

Johnny tipped back his hat. "I had to. There were some important people here."

"Mom and me?"

Johnny sobered. "I shouldn't have left you, Brady. I made you a promise and I wasn't keeping it."

"It's not the cowboy way," the kid reminded him.

Johnny worked up a smile. "No, it's not. The important thing was I should have been there for you and I wasn't. I promise I won't do that again."

His blue eyes rounded. "You're gonna stay?"

"I want to, but first there are a lot of things I have to make up for."

"Grown-up things, huh?"

"Yeah." He looked at Jess and she felt her chest tighten with emotion. "I let a lot of people down."

Brady looked back at her. "Mom, are you still mad at Johnny?"

Jess couldn't talk about this right now. She needed a minute just to absorb the fact the man came back.

"Brady, that's something Johnny and I need to talk about later. Right now you better decide if you're going to ride or not."

"If Johnny will, I will."

"No, Brady, you can't do that," Johnny told him. "Either you want to ride in this parade, or not. If you get on a horse it's your choice."

He glanced up at Jess, then back at Brady. "Think about it, I need to talk to your mom."

The boy nodded. "You better say something nice because she's really sad."

Johnny walked a few feet away and Jess followed. Her heart was pounding so hard, she couldn't hear anything else. "I can't imagine what else you have to say to me...."

"There's a lot, Jess. I can't ask you to forgive me right off, but will you give me a chance to explain things?"

She was afraid. "Johnny, I'm not sure I can do this again."

"I know I walked out on you and Brady. But I actually thought it was for the best. Then I realized I don't want a life without you." He glanced toward the arena. "I'm asking for another chance, to try and explain things, later. Right now, I want to make this day special for your son. Will you trust me enough to do that?"

Jess tried to say no, but she saw something in this man. He'd been hurt as a child so she knew he wouldn't intentionally hurt Brady. "Okay."

He smiled. "Another question, will you let him ride with me on Storm?"

She immediately felt panicked, but she quickly realized she trusted this man not to endanger her son. "I don't have a problem, but Brady might."

"Thanks, you won't regret it. Let's get this rodeo started off right."

Johnny went outside and took Storm from the trailer, then walked him inside to the railing. He hoped he could pull this off. All the others were seated on their horses and lined up for the opening ceremony.

Brady saw him, too. "Okay, son. You ready?"

"You gonna ride Storm?"

"We're gonna ride him," he corrected. "Your grandfather loved Storm, and now you love him. He won't hurt you, you know that. And I'll be there right with you."

The boy nodded.

Johnny glanced at Derrick and Cheyenne looking

somewhat dubious over the choice of mount. "Come on, let's show Tucker how a Calhoun does it."

Brady gave him a high five. "Okay!"

Johnny lifted the boy up into the saddle, then climbed on behind him. Storm did a little sideways dance, but obeyed Johnny's commands and got back in the line.

A big grin lit up Brady's face as one of the officials handed him the Texas flag to carry and Jess climbed on Goldie and moved in beside them. Johnny wanted to reach over and kiss her, but knew he didn't have that right anymore.

The music started and they headed to the arena together as the crowd cheered.

"I wish Grandpa was here," Brady said.

"He is, son. He's looking down on you right now."

Over the next few hours, the day's events and commitments kept them apart, and Jess realized it was a good thing. Given some time maybe she could figure out if she was happy about Johnny's return.

She glanced at the man spending time with her son. When he turned and caught her staring, he winked and smiled at her. Okay, yes, she was more than happy he came back. At least he deserved a chance to be heard. But what about the future?

He walked toward her. "I'm sorry, Jess. I want to talk with you, to tell you so many things." He glanced around at the crowd of people. "Oh, hell." He pulled her into his arms and his mouth captured hers. She didn't have a chance to protest, not that she wanted to. Being in Johnny's arms was heaven to her. He pulled back slowly as those gray eyes searched her face. "God, I missed you, Jess. There's so much I need to say to you, but I'd like to do it when I have more time…and privacy."

She felt giddy. "I'd like to hear what you have to say, too."

"Good." He grinned as he stepped back. "First, I have a little boy who wants to win a buckle today."

"Then go do it." She grabbed his hand to stop him. "We're a package deal, Johnny."

He cupped her face in his hands. "If you don't know it yet, Jess Calhoun, I love you both, and want to be a part of your lives. I'd be a lucky man if you shared Brady with me."

She blinked back the tears. "Consider yourself a lucky man."

He kissed her again. "Hold that thought and I'll be back." He took off and she fought to keep from running after him. Instead, she went to the side bleachers and sat down, still reeling from Johnny's kiss and his promises.

Molly dropped down beside her. "Well, it seems your cowboy has come back in a big way."

"Yep, he has."

Her friend nodded and gripped her hand as Brady shot out of the chute, riding a sheep.

She jumped to her feet, cheering. "Go, Brady." She watched as he hung on until the buzzer went off. The child let go and dropped to the ground. Then suddenly her son was on his feet, brushing off his jeans. Johnny hurried toward him and lifted the smiling Brady up into the air. They both raised their arms seeing the time on the scoreboard.

"He won," Molly cheered. "He won!"

Jess watched the man holding her son and all her doubts disappeared. "We both won."

Hours later, Johnny carried the sleeping boy up the stairs and he laid him down on his bed at the ranch as he'd done before. But tonight he wanted it to be his regular job.

He stared down at the boy, seeing the big buckle that adorned his waist. Pride filled him, knowing how hard the boy had worked to get it.

He started to remove the boy's clothes, but suddenly Brady woke up and stopped him. "No! I want to wear my belt. Please."

Jess came in with pajamas. "I think he'll be fine for tonight." She kissed her son and walked out.

Johnny hung back and helped dress the boy. "Brady, I need to ask you something."

He yawned. "What?"

Johnny sat down on the bed. "How do you feel about me staying here?"

"Like forever?"

Johnny realized how much it meant to him if Brady wanted him in his life. He nodded. "I hurt your mom and you. I'm sorry."

"It's okay, you came back. That means you love us. Do you want to be my dad?"

He was struck by the insight this kid had. "Yes, I do. I want us to be a family."

"Then maybe you should ask his mother first," he heard a familiar voice say.

He turned to see Jess standing in the dim light. Brady nudged him. "Go say nice things to Mom."

Johnny kissed the boy. "I think I can handle this on my own," he said, but he wasn't so sure.

He stood and went to Jess. He took her by the arm and directed her out into the hall and closed the door. "Is there somewhere we can talk?"

Jess took his hand and led him down the hall to her old bedroom. She didn't even turn on the lights. The moon gave off enough light for her to see his silhouette.

"For a man who was anxious to talk, you sure took your sweet time."

She gasped when Johnny reached for her and his mouth came down on hers. She sank into his embrace and gave in to all the pent-up feelings inside her. He'd come back to her. He loved her.

He broke off the kiss and stepped back. "Whoa, sorry, I really wanted to talk to you first. To tell you I was crazy to drive away yesterday. I know I hurt you and I'm so sorry." He turned away and went to the large window. "I've never been part of a real family, Jess. You know about my mom and me, and those weren't the best times. I took off at fourteen. I've been on my own for so long, depending only on myself, I was afraid to trust. I was afraid to let myself care about another person."

Jess heard the pain in his voice as he poured out his feelings. She couldn't have loved him more.

"I'm not sure I'd be any good at it now." He drew a breath and released it. "But damn, you and Brady make me want to try." He came to her. "I want to belong here, Jess. I love you. I love you so much. I want us to be a family. To put down roots and build a home, have more kids." He hesitated, then said, "Please give us a chance."

She slipped her arms around his middle and looked up at him. "You're right, it hurt me when you left, but it doesn't change the fact that I love you, Johnny Jameson. And I always will."

He let out a breath. "Oh, God. I love you. I plan to tell you every day." He paused. "That is if you'll do me the honor of becoming my wife."

"Oh, Johnny." She touched his face. "Are you sure?"

"I've never been so sure of anything. I think the first time I saw you, I was drawn to you, not just because you're the prettiest woman I've ever met, but I've felt this connection. I could talk to you, share with you. You made me feel like I belong."

Johnny pulled her close. "I know I've always traveled from ranch to ranch with my training, but how would you feel if I headquartered my operation here at the Double Bar C?"

"Oh, Johnny, that's perfect."

"Besides the fact that I'm suddenly tired of traveling around the country, your bakery is here. There are your plans for the expansion, and I hope not just the business. I want a real family, Jess. I didn't know how much until I found you. I love Brady and I want to adopt him so I can be his real father. If that's okay with you?"

Jess couldn't speak, the emotions clogged her throat. She nodded.

He took her hands. "If you're willing, I want us to

have another child, too. And I will be at your side, loving you more seeing our baby grow in you."

She touched his handsome face. "I see you've been doing a lot of thinking about this."

He brushed his lips across hers. "It was a long drive back from the state line."

"I guess so."

"I know I've given you a long list of things I want, but in truth all I need is you and Brady."

"And I need you." She kissed him sweetly. "I can't wait to start our lives together."

"There is one catch," he said. "I have a commitment in Florida, but I want you and Brady to go with me. It's only temporary, a few months at most. It's warm there, and I know you have the bakery, but I'm sure Molly could look after things—"

Jess pulled his head down and covered his mouth with hers. Didn't he realize that she would change her world for this man? "I'll go wherever you go. Would you mind taking a five-year-old on a honeymoon?"

She felt his grin. "Oh, darlin', our honeymoon isn't ever going to end."

"Oh, Johnny, I like the way you think, but don't make any promises you can't keep."

He brushed his mouth over hers. "I can promise you this, Jess. I'll always love you and Brady. I will treat him as my own son. I swear you can depend on me to stick around."

She smiled, feeling tears threatening again. "Because it's the cowboy way?"

"It's my way, and my promise to you."

His mouth closed over hers, sealing the deal. She

knew this man would make her life complete, and Johnny had her love and, most important, a home. Together the next generation would live and prosper on Calhoun land.

EPILOGUE

IN TWO days Jess was going to get married. Some would say it was too soon, but she had no doubts about becoming Mrs. Johnny Jameson.

The wedding wasn't going to be big. That was how she and Johnny wanted it. With her parents gone, and the rest of her family not able to make it home for the ceremony, it was just as well. She'd have family, though, Molly and her mom and dad, along with Wes and Nancy and maybe some friends from town. Molly was her maid of honor, and Johnny had chosen Brady to stand up for him.

"I can't believe we're pulling off a wedding in just forty-eight hours," she said as Johnny walked into the ranch kitchen. She stood at the counter looking over her to-do list. The wedding would be in the front parlor, and the reception in the dining room.

He came up behind her and wrapped his arms around her. He kissed her on the neck, sending shivers down her spine. "As far as I'm concerned, brown eyes, it isn't soon enough."

She loved his husky voice. "You're saying that because you only have to show up."

Johnny smiled at his soon-to-be bride. That wasn't

exactly true. He'd found an engagement ring that was perfect for Jess. An antique sapphire ring surrounded with tiny diamonds.

When he'd given it to her two nights ago, she began to cry. His heart nearly stopped until she told him they were tears of joy. He'd also arranged for a house to stay in during his temporary employment at Ransen Stables in the Florida panhandle. He figured two months tops, they'd be home to Texas.

"I've found us a place to live."

She smiled. "That's good. It's not a hotel, is it?"

"Actually, it's more of a cottage, a two-bedroom at the ranch. So Brady will have his own room and you and I will have ours." He turned her around and kissed her again. He could easily get lost in this woman, and forget about this wedding. Yet for the first time in his life he wanted to be committed to another person. To put down roots here, and the first step was marriage. So before things got out of hand, he pulled back.

They were both trying to catch their breath when Jess said, "I can't believe this is happening. It's like a dream, Johnny. If so, don't wake me up."

He knew the feeling. He also knew how lucky he'd been to find Jess. "Oh, darlin'. If I don't wake you up, you'll miss all the fun."

Jess stepped back from temptation, and Johnny Jameson was definitely that. "Stop distracting me. I have too much to do."

The wedding day was going to be a little bittersweet, too. Her mother wasn't here to advise her, and her father couldn't give her away. Maybe that was why she was so eager to find something of her mother's today.

"What can I do to help you?"

"How do you feel about digging through some boxes?"

He arched an eyebrow. "What are we looking for?"

"Something old."

He frowned.

"You know the saying, 'something old, something new, something borrowed and something blue.' I already have my dress and that's new." She smiled, recalling her trip to San Antonio to find a satin-and-lace garden-length dress.

"I have something blue." She'd bought a blue garter. "I borrowed a pair of earrings from Molly. So now I need something old." She swallowed back the sudden emotions. "From my mother."

Johnny smiled. "Do you know what you want?"

She nodded. "I'm just not sure where it is. That's why I might need a big, strong guy like you to move some boxes." She took his hand and pulled him with her up the steps.

"Are you sure you want to search through boxes when we have the evening to ourselves? After about three hours of riding today, I'm sure Brady isn't getting up tonight for anything."

Johnny drew Jess into his arms and covered her mouth in a passionate kiss. He was more than ready to carry his future bride off for a little prehoneymoon. In the past week they'd been getting ready for the wedding, and spending time with Brady. He'd been feeling a little neglected.

Not that he didn't love that kid, but he needed one-on-one time with his mother, especially since Jess had asked him if they could hold off from making love until their wedding night.

She smiled and placed a teasing kiss on his mouth. "Just think how good it will be for us in two nights. I promise to make it worth the wait."

"You better stop teasing me, Ms. Calhoun, or you'll be in trouble."

She grinned. "Come on, I'll distract you with the search."

She pulled him along the hall. She hadn't been in here since they cleared out her father's clothes and sent them off to the church thrift store.

She walked into her parents' bedroom and was hit with a flood of memories. She pushed them aside, knowing her parents wouldn't want her to be sad. They'd want her to be happy starting her new life with Johnny.

Jess hurried through the large room and went into the big walk-in closet. It was still filled with boxes of their parents' things they hadn't had the heart to get rid of.

Johnny stopped at the doorway. "Don't tell me we're going through all of this."

"I'm hoping what I'm looking for is in my mother's jewelry case." Sandra Calhoun's cameo pin was Jess's favorite and would be perfect for her wedding dress.

"We might just need to move some boxes."

She walked toward the back until she found the small dresser. She located it behind several cartons. Johnny moved them for her and she began going through the dainty drawers, one by one. They were mostly filled with stationery. There was also a collection of cards and letters from friends and family.

"Bingo," she said as she pulled out a small wooden box. After searching through several pieces of jewelry, she found the cameo pin. It looked old with its antique gold edging and the simple silhouette in the center. "It's perfect."

"Did you find it?" Johnny asked.

"Yes." She pocketed the pin, then closed the box. She went to slip the box back into the drawer when she saw an envelope. She picked up the aged linen paper and saw that it was addressed to her dad.

"What is this doing in Mom's things?"

Johnny looked over her shoulder. "What else did you find?"

"I'm not sure." She stood and walked out into the bedroom for more light. With her father's recent death, she wasn't sure if this was important or not.

She turned on the bedside lamp and sank down onto the bed. Johnny stood in the middle of the room as she examined the back side of the envelope. "It was posted in New York."

"I'm sure your dad had business dealings everywhere. Why not New York?"

She eyed the postmark. "Oh, my God! This was mailed thirty years ago."

Johnny nodded. "Well, it's a little late if they want an answer."

"Should I open it?"

With his nod, she realized the seal hadn't been broken. With a slight hesitation, Jess studied the yellowed paper, then she gently pried the seal off and carefully opened it. She pulled out the single page and unfolded it. A strange feeling engulfed her the second she began to read.

Dear Clay,
Leaving you broke my heart but we both know it was for the best. Even so, every day I think of you and what might have been. I've met someone else now, and he's helping me get myself back to-gether. We're getting married, Clay.

And there's something else. Something I can barely bring myself to write, although I know you have to know. I'm pregnant, Clay, pregnant with your twins! We both thought this could never be possible, but now it seems that nature has worked its miracle, but all too late.

I want you to know your children. Even if we can't be together. Clay, when you get this, please write back to me. It doesn't have to be over for us.

Forever yours,
Fenella

Jess felt her heart pounding hard against her rib cage. As if Johnny saw her stress, he sat down be-side her and together they read over the words on the page. The words that would change the Calhoun fam-ily forever.

* * * * *

Mills & Boon® Hardback

August 2012

ROMANCE

Contract with Consequences	Miranda Lee
The Sheikh's Last Gamble	Trish Morey
The Man She Shouldn't Crave	Lucy Ellis
The Girl He'd Overlooked	Cathy Williams
A Tainted Beauty	Sharon Kendrick
One Night With The Enemy	Abby Green
The Dangerous Jacob Wilde	Sandra Marton
His Last Chance at Redemption	Michelle Conder
The Hidden Heart of Rico Rossi	Kate Hardy
Marrying the Enemy	Nicola Marsh
Mr Right, Next Door!	Barbara Wallace
The Cowboy Comes Home	Patricia Thayer
The Rancher's Housekeeper	Rebecca Winters
Her Outback Rescuer	Marion Lennox
Monsoon Wedding Fever	Shoma Narayanan
If the Ring Fits...	Jackie Braun
Sydney Harbour Hospital: Ava's Re-Awakening	Carol Marinelli
How To Mend A Broken Heart	Amy Andrews

MEDICAL

Falling for Dr Fearless	Lucy Clark
The Nurse He Shouldn't Notice	Susan Carlisle
Every Boy's Dream Dad	Sue MacKay
Return of the Rebel Surgeon	Connie Cox

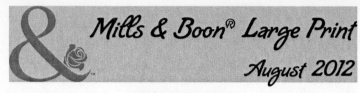

Mills & Boon® Large Print

August 2012

ROMANCE

A Deal at the Altar	Lynne Graham
Return of the Moralis Wife	Jacqueline Baird
Gianni's Pride	Kim Lawrence
Undone by His Touch	Annie West
The Cattle King's Bride	Margaret Way
New York's Finest Rebel	Trish Wylie
The Man Who Saw Her Beauty	Michelle Douglas
The Last Real Cowboy	Donna Alward
The Legend of de Marco	Abby Green
Stepping out of the Shadows	Robyn Donald
Deserving of His Diamonds?	Melanie Milburne

HISTORICAL

The Scandalous Lord Lanchester	Anne Herries
Highland Rogue, London Miss	Margaret Moore
His Compromised Countess	Deborah Hale
The Dragon and the Pearl	Jeannie Lin
Destitute On His Doorstep	Helen Dickson

MEDICAL

Sydney Harbour Hospital: Lily's Scandal	Marion Lennox
Sydney Harbour Hospital: Zoe's Baby	Alison Roberts
Gina's Little Secret	Jennifer Taylor
Taming the Lone Doc's Heart	Lucy Clark
The Runaway Nurse	Dianne Drake
The Baby Who Saved Dr Cynical	Connie Cox

Mills & Boon® Hardback

September 2012

ROMANCE

MEDICAL

Mills & Boon® Large Print

September 2012

ROMANCE

A Vow of Obligation	Lynne Graham
Defying Drakon	Carole Mortimer
Playing the Greek's Game	Sharon Kendrick
One Night in Paradise	Maisey Yates
Valtieri's Bride	Caroline Anderson
The Nanny Who Kissed Her Boss	Barbara McMahon
Falling for Mr Mysterious	Barbara Hannay
The Last Woman He'd Ever Date	Liz Fielding
His Majesty's Mistake	Jane Porter
Duty and the Beast	Trish Morey
The Darkest of Secrets	Kate Hewitt

HISTORICAL

Lady Priscilla's Shameful Secret	Christine Merrill
Rake with a Frozen Heart	Marguerite Kaye
Miss Cameron's Fall from Grace	Helen Dickson
Society's Most Scandalous Rake	Isabelle Goddard
The Taming of the Rogue	Amanda McCabe

MEDICAL

Falling for the Sheikh She Shouldn't	Fiona McArthur
Dr Cinderella's Midnight Fling	Kate Hardy
Brought Together by Baby	Margaret McDonagh
One Month to Become a Mum	Louisa George
Sydney Harbour Hospital: Luca's Bad Girl	Amy Andrews
The Firebrand Who Unlocked His Heart	Anne Fraser